THE SECRET OF GABI'S DRESSER

The Secret of
Gabi's Dresser

by

KATHY KACER

SECOND
STORY
Press

CANADIAN CATALOGUING IN PUBLICATION DATA

Kacer, Kathy, 1954–
The secret of Gabi's dresser

ISBN 1-896764-15-0

I. Jewish children in the Holocaust – Juvenile fiction.
2. Holocaust, Jewish (1939-1945) - Juvenile fiction. I. Title.

PS8571.A33S42 1999   jC813'.54   C99-930306-6
PZ7.K1155Se 1999

Cover illustration by Linda Montgomery

*Second Story Press gratefully acknowledges the assistance of the
Ontario Arts Council and the Canada Council for the Arts
for our publishing program. We acknowledge the financial
support of the Government of Canada through the
Book Publishing Industry Development Program.*

Printed and bound in Canada

Published by
SECOND STORY PRESS
*720 Bathurst Street, Suite 301
Toronto, Canada M5S 2R4*

DEDICATION

In memory of my late mother, Gabriela Offenberg Kacer,
with deep love and admiration.

For my children, Gabi and Jake. It is up to them
to carry the memory forward.

ACKNOWLEDGEMENTS

My gratitude goes to Margie Wolfe and Second Story
Press for having faith in a new author, to Sarah Swartz
for helping me get started and to Gena Gorrell
for her insightful feedback.

I am blessed with the love and support of my husband
and children, Ian Epstein, Gabi and Jake. Their
encouragement and enthusiasm have inspired me
to realize my dream of writing.

Foreword

IN 1933 the Nazi party took power in Germany, led by Adolf Hitler, a powerful and ruthless dictator who crushed anyone who opposed him. The Nazis believed that most Germans were part of a superior Aryan race, and the "inferior" people such as Jews, gypsies and the disabled should be eliminated. Under Nazi rule, Jews were blamed for Germany's defeat in the First World War and for the country's terrible economic problems.

In March 1938, Germany occupied neighbouring Austria. Italy, Hungary and Romania sided with the Nazis. In September 1938, Hitler was handed part of Czechoslovakia as part of the "Munich Pact," an agreement with Great Britain, France and Italy. Within six months most of Czechoslovakia was under Nazi domination.

On September 1, 1939, Germany invaded Poland, and the Second World War began. As country after country fell to the German army — Denmark, Norway, France, Belgium, Holland — the persecution of Jews spread across almost all of Europe. Jewish people were oppressed by endless rules and regulations. They lost their jobs, and their homes and belongings were stolen. They were forced into camps and used as slave labour, or starved, or simply murdered.

Germany and its supporters — known as the Axis — were opposed by the Allies, countries including Great Britain, Canada, Australia, New Zealand, and later the United States and the Soviet Union. The Allies won the war, but by the time Germany was defeated, in May 1945, at least six million Jews and many other innocent people had been murdered, in the name of the "superior" Aryan race.

Chapter One

"HOME FREE!" cried Vera, as she ran past Paul and touched the staircase. She bounced up and down, dancing around her brother as she shouted, "You're *it* again!"

"Where were you hiding this time?" demanded Paul, a frustrated look on his face. "I searched everywhere."

"Now, why would I tell you that?" teased Vera. "I might want to hide there again." She could see how annoyed her brother was, but it was fun to taunt him this way.

"Aw, no fair, Vera. There are too many places to hide in this house. I don't want to be *it* all the time."

Vera and Paul were at their grandmother's house. Their parents dropped them there every Sunday before lunch and came back to pick them up before supper.

Their grandmother lived in an old house in the centre of the city. She often complained that the three-storey house was far too big for one person. There were too many staircases, too many out-of-the-way rooms, too many nooks and crannies. But for Vera and Paul the house was a perfect place for hide-and-seek.

"Let's see," said Vera. "I hid five times and you only caught me once. Let's play one more time, and then go get something to eat."

"Okay, once more, but this time — YOU'RE *IT*!" Paul knocked her on the arm and ran off, shrieking with delight.

"No way! I won the last round! Paul, you're a cheater," shouted Vera chasing after her brother and grabbing him by the shoulder.

At that moment, their grandmother appeared in the kitchen doorway. She had been baking and her hands were covered with cookie dough and held up in front of her, as if she were a doctor who had just scrubbed for surgery. Her apron, a gift from her grandchildren, was splattered with flour, sugar and other ingredients. Its pale blue and red flowers were coated in a dusting of icing sugar that trailed from her shoulders down to the top of her knees, where the apron ended. Using the back of one hand, she carefully pushed her glasses back up on her nose.

"Vera! Paul! So much noise! This is not a playground. The neighbours must think there is a circus going on in here." Although her voice sounded harsh, Vera and Paul knew that she wasn't really annoyed. She was never angry with them — at least, not for long.

"Babichka, Paul is cheating," began Vera, still holding her brother by the arm.

"I am not," interrupted Paul, struggling to free himself from his sister's grasp. "You're the one who won't play fair!"

"Children, children, stop! You both know better than to fight like this. I was just coming to tell you that I have poppyseed cookies and walnut cake coming out of the oven. But if you would rather stay here and argue, I'm sure I can find someone else to eat them." Her eyes twinkled as she tempted them with their favourite treats.

"Forget fighting," said Paul. "I'm hungry!" Both children laughed as they followed their grandmother into the kitchen, the argument forgotten.

It seemed as if their babichka's kitchen always smelled of good things. Sometimes there were mealtime smells like veal, roasted with whole potatoes and carrots. But on Sundays there were usually dessert smells like the ones now coming out of the oven. Vera and Paul watched as their grandmother carefully cut the walnut cake and placed a slice in front of each of them with a glass of milk. Cinnamon and raisins oozed from each piece. The children wasted no time in polishing off their servings and asking for seconds.

"Mmmmm, this is the best," said Vera with a sigh.

Gabi Kohn gazed lovingly at her grandchildren. Having them visit every Sunday was the highlight of her week. She always looked forward to baking, playing games and sharing stories with them. At seventy years of age she was attractive and always beautifully dressed, with her silver grey hair pulled back in a neatly combed bun. She had always been short, and was rounder than she had once been, but she carried herself with dignity and elegance. Her bright green eyes and lively manner still made her seem young.

"I'm glad you like the cake, my darlings. And now that your stomachs are full, tell me what on earth you were fighting over."

"Well, it's simple," began Paul. "The problem is, this house has too many hiding places. Every time Vera goes to hide, I can never find her, so I have to be it over and over again. It's impossible to find anybody in this house."

Their grandmother looked thoughtful. "Did I ever tell you about the very special hiding place that I once had?"

Vera and Paul smiled, sensing a story. Their grandmother told wonderful stories, and they loved to spend their Sundays listening to her. Sometimes she read them stories from books, and her voice would change with each new character. She could sound old and spooky like the scariest witch, or as young and playful as a child. She could even do voices for different animals.

Often she invented magical stories out of her own mind. She made up stories about enchanted, far-off places with people who had exciting adventures but always managed to live happily ever after.

But the stories that Vera and Paul liked best were the ones she told about her childhood. These stories were about real people, and adventures that actually happened. Through their grandmother's stories, Vera and Paul had been introduced to family and events they had never known. It was like looking through a window into their own past.

"Did you play hide-and-seek when you were little?" asked Paul. "You know, when you were growing up in Czecho ... Czechos ..."

"Cze-cho-slo-va-ki-a," Vera said carefully. She was ten years old, two years older than her brother. She could often remember things that were difficult for him.

"Yeah, Czechoslovakia," said Paul, frowning at her interruption.

"Well, I was close to your age when I had my hiding place. But this was a time when I was not playing," replied their babichka, as she closed her eyes and sat back in her chair. Vera and Paul knew that she was thinking about her childhood. Often, when she started a story about her home-land, she would pause, as if her thoughts had drifted, many years and many miles away. She had always been honest with them about her life in Europe in the 1930s and 1940s, even about how her family and others had suf-fered as Jews. Vera and Paul waited patiently for her to start talking again.

"Come with me, children," she said abruptly, as she rose out of her chair. "I'd like to show you something."

They followed her as she lead them out of the kitchen and into the living room. In the centre of the room was a wooden dresser. The children had never paid much atten-tion to it before — it was just there, like any other piece of furniture in the room. Now they watched as their grandmother ran her fingers lovingly across the top of the dresser. Its wood, though cracked in several places, was polished to a soft shine that made the dresser glow in the afternoon light. The outside of the dresser was carved with elaborate decorations. On its top, on hand-embroidered doilies, sat two crystal candy bowls, a porcelain statue of two children sitting on a park bench and a photograph of Vera, Paul and their parents. Their grandmother reached into one of the crystal bowls and drew out an old metal key. She bent and unlocked both doors of the dresser.

"This dresser sat in the dining room of the house where I lived when I was a child," she began. "My mother kept beautiful things inside. She kept her fine crystal, perfect white china with a gold rim, and silverware that was polished until it shone, that we used only for special occasions."

"Those are just like the things you have in there now," interrupted Paul.

"Let Babichka tell her story," protested Vera.

The old woman paused as the children settled comfortably on the couch. "Yes, just like me, my mother kept beautiful things in the dresser. But there was a time when all these lovely things were taken out and put away. Then the dresser was used for something different. This dresser was my secret hiding place."

Chapter Two

MANY, MANY YEARS AGO, I lived with my parents on a farm, in a small village in the eastern part of the country that was then called Czechoslovakia. We had a fine old stone house with beautiful rooms, shiny wooden floors and a twisting spiral staircase. When I looked out my bedroom window, I could see the mountains that surrounded our land and separated us from Poland. The mountains changed with each season, as if an artist had created a brand-new painting. In winter they were frosty and white with snow, and bare bushes and trees cast deep blue and grey shadows across the hillside. In summer, as wild roses and yellow dandelions bloomed across the mountains, they were splashed with a rainbow of colours.

I didn't really know it at the time, but this was a critical period in Czechoslovakia's history and indeed in the history of the world. There was a war beginning in Germany, and it was slowly creeping its way towards us. It would have a devastating impact on people everywhere, particularly Jews like us. But as a child I was protected from this knowledge, at least for a while. For me, my country was a safe and secure place to live. And I was cared for and loved in my home.

There were other Jewish families in our village and villages close by, though not many of them were farmers. Most of them owned businesses. The Bottensteins had a clothing shop; Mr. Wohl owned the lumberyard; the Deutch family were tailors. Within our Jewish community there was one doctor, one lawyer and one pharmacist. Other Jewish families were shopkeepers, selling textiles, food, pots and pans and farming equipment. On evenings and weekends, Mr. Schlesinger, the owner of the local pub, played host to my father and his friends, who could often be found playing cards, drinking coffee and catching up on the local gossip. My favourite place was the bakery, where Mrs. Springer would sometimes give cupcakes to my friends and me when we passed.

Our farm was one of the largest in the area. We grew wheat, oats, barley and potatoes, and raised dairy cattle. We had many workers who helped take care of the cows and the fields. My father worked the land and managed the farm. My mother took care of our home and helped my father wherever she was needed. There was nothing she could not or would not do. She gathered crops along with the workers. She tended the animals when they were sick or giving birth. She even knew about human diseases and medicines. The workers on our farm would often come to her for advice if they were ill, rather than travel into town to see the doctor. I took part in all these farm activities, and I grew up sharing my parents' love for the land.

I remember the time I stayed up all night long to watch a cow give birth. My mother let me stroke the cow's head while she helped deliver the calf. I watched in amazement as the head, shoulders and legs of the baby emerged from its mother. I named the calf Tibi, and he followed me around the barn like a puppy.

Our village was too small to have a school of its own so, until I was twelve years old, I attended a school in the town next to ours. Each day my friends and I would walk for more than half an hour to get to school. We didn't mind the walk because we had so much fun talking together. The time passed quickly with our stories and games.

"Gabi," my friend Marishka would call to me, "do you want to race to school?"

"No, don't run," Nettie would complain. "My shoes are new and they're pinching my toes."

"Oh, poor thing. New shoes, a new dress, new ribbons in your hair. But you can't even walk," we would tease. Nettie's parents owned the fanciest dress shop in town, and her clothes were always the latest style. Sometimes she brought us special things from the store; a silk scarf for me, a colourful ribbon for Marishka's hair, even a hand-made handkerchief for one of the boys.

"Gabi, will you come with me to the bakery after school? I have some extra allowance, and I'll treat you to a chocolate roll," Nina said one day. Nina was my best friend. We lived on neighbouring farms and we had grown up together. Unlike most of my friends, Nina was not Jewish. I listened to her tempt me with my favourite dessert and realized that, once again, she had forgotten something important in my life. It was Friday. I had to go straight home after school to help prepare the house for the sabbath.

"I'd love to, but I have to set the table before sunset," I reminded her.

"Oops, I forgot. It's not fair that you can't play on Fridays. Especially in winter, when it gets dark so fast we never have enough time to do anything."

"Maybe Mamma will let you sleep over next Friday night," I suggested. "You can come home with me after school and help get things ready. Remember the last Friday night you came? I'll bet you can't remember the Hebrew blessing we taught you."

"At least I'll remember not to blow out the sabbath candles after supper. How was I supposed to know they're meant to burn all the way down?"

Nina and I laughed as we held hands and walked together. We had always been like sisters, and we shared our biggest secrets. The difference in our religions didn't get in the way of our friendship. We were just curious about each other's traditions and holidays. I remember once going to holy communion at the Catholic church in town. Nina and her parents explained to me what it meant when they drank the red wine and ate the small biscuit the priest offered. I felt closer to Nina after that, as if we had shared something very private. I knew she felt the same way when she came to our house for Passover. She tasted matzo, the unleavened bread, for the first time. And she helped read aloud parts of the Passover story, as if she were my very own sister.

It wasn't like that with all the Christian families in town. Many of these people looked at the Jews with a combination of resentment and fear. They envied any success Jewish people had in business, and they were afraid and suspicious of anyone who practised a different religion. There were some who made trouble for us, not shopping in stores owned by Jewish merchants, writing nasty messages on the synagogue wall, or not letting their children play with us. The very religious Jews were the target of most of these incidents because they looked so different — the men wore long black coats and black hats, and their wives covered their heads with wigs and wore plain-coloured dresses that covered their arms and legs and were usually buttoned up tight to their necks. They spoke mostly Yiddish, and their children attended special schools that emphasized religious studies. My school had a mixture of Christian and Jewish children, and I suppose that's how you could describe our home too. It was mixed with religious customs and not so religious ones.

For example, we followed strict dietary laws. There were some foods we never ate, and we didn't have meat and dairy products in the same meal. We even had two sets of dishes, one for meat, one for milk. But we didn't go to synagogue every sabbath, and sometimes my father worked on the day set aside for rest. While we observed many Jewish customs and holidays, we weren't as religious as the most observant Jews, and we didn't dress the way they did. Perhaps that was why I could mix so easily with my Christian schoolmates.

Some of my friends weren't so lucky. One group of Christian boys had a reputation for picking fights with the Jewish boys in my school. My friend David was cornered by them one day. They tried to force him to hand over some money. When he refused, they jumped on him, trying to punch and kick him and rip his clothes. David managed to stand up to them, and even landed a few punches himself before he got away. He ended up with a black eye but he wore it proudly, pleased that he had stood up for himself. Incidents like this happened occasionally. When they did, the grown-ups usually just shrugged their shoulders and said there wasn't much we could do except ignore the bullies. We learned to avoid situations that might lead to trouble.

That Friday afternoon, I said goodbye to Nina and we promised to go ice skating the next evening on the frozen pond. I turned to walk up the long road to my house. I wasn't really sorry I couldn't go to the bakery. I looked forward to the sabbath more than any other day of the week. On Fridays, by the time I returned from school, our house was already filled with the smells of my mother's cooking.

A fragrance of chicken soup, yeasty egg bread and apple strudel surrounded me as soon as I walked in the door.

"Mamma," I shouted as I burst in. "I have to tell you what happened at school today. Mr. Reich was bending over Nina's desk to correct her arithmetic and when he stood up he knocked over the inkwell. He spilled black ink all over his suit. Everyone laughed so hard, except Mr. Reich, of course, and ..."

"Gabi, slow down and take a moment to breathe," my mother replied, holding my cold cheeks between her warm hands. "I want to hear all your stories, but first get the china and silver from the dresser and set the table. Then prepare the sabbath candles for lighting. It will soon be dark, and your father will be home from work."

The dresser sat in the dining room, and it held all our special things. Each Friday I took the metal key that my mother kept hanging in the kitchen and unlocked its two doors. First I found the white linen tablecloth and matching napkins that my mother had embroidered with her initials. Then I carefully removed the white china and the silver candlesticks. The crystal glasses were the last to be carried from the dresser to the table. I was painfully careful not to drop anything. A crack in a plate, a chip in a glass or a dent in the silver would have been heartbreaking, both for me and for my mother. I cherished these treasures as if they were my own. And I loved the wooden dresser that housed them.

Chapter Three

FRIDAY EVENINGS were always the same in our home. From the moment I stepped in the door until the time I went to bed, I could rely on our routine as I relied on the sun rising and setting each day. I waited by the staircase for my father's return from work. I listened for the sound of the door opening, and his footsteps in the hallway. Then I threw myself into his arms as soon as he had taken off his jacket.

"Ah, my Gabi, how you startled me! I didn't expect you to be there," my father joked each week, as he enclosed me in his powerful arms for a hug. He always smelled like pipe smoke mixed with shaving lotion. I loved this familiar scent.

"Papa, I have to tell you what we did at school today." My stories began the moment my father arrived home. "Remember the story I wrote about how I watched our calf being born last spring? Well, I got the highest mark in my class. And I got to read it out loud to everyone. And then later in the day Nina handed out invitations to her birthday party, and Mamma says she'll take me to town next week so we can buy Nina a present. I saw some beautiful writing paper I think she'd love, and ..."

"Gabi, slow down and give me a chance to sit down. Sabbath will be over and I'll still be standing here listening to your stories. There will be lots of time to talk during supper."

Our house was bustling as the sabbath dinner was prepared. Some of the workers helped Mamma make supper in the kitchen, while Papa read the newspaper and rested from his long workday. I ran between them, sometimes helping Mamma cook, sometimes interrupting Papa's reading, and probably getting in the way a lot!

Just before sunset, my father put on his yarmulka, the skullcap worn for prayers and meals, and we lit the sabbath candles, in the silver candlesticks I had taken from the dresser. These candlesticks had belonged to my great-grandmother and had been passed down to my grandmother and to my mother. Mamma reminded me each Friday evening that some day they would be passed on to me, so that I could continue our traditions. I lit the candles and Mamma and I covered our eyes as we recited the sabbath blessing in Hebrew. Papa always whispered a quiet prayer under his breath. He said it was a special blessing to keep all of us safe. I felt very secure standing there with my parents, in the soft glow of the candlelight.

Then it was time to eat. Even our meal was the same each week. We started with chicken soup and fluffy dumplings the shape of clouds. Next, we feasted on roast chicken and beef, sweet potatoes and carrots, and fried apple dumplings. The roast chicken was still sizzling when my mother brought it to the table. I always asked for the wings and crunched the bones. Our meal ended with cinnamon raisin cake that was sweet and hot. If I was lucky, I got to have seconds of everything. I even got a sip of Papa's wine.

Sometimes we were joined by other members of our family. Although I was an only child, I had many aunts, uncles and cousins. When they came for the sabbath, our house was a frenzy of noise and activity. On those nights, we children ate at a smaller table in the kitchen, away from the grown-ups. Although it was fun to be on our own, pretending that this was our private dinner party, I didn't always like having to look after my younger cousins. I was the one who got into trouble if they misbehaved! Like the time little Mira opened the dresser and started playing with my mother's crystal flower vase. By the time I noticed that Mira had it in her hands, it was too late. I watched, helpless, as the glass crashed to the ground. Mamma blamed me, saying it was my responsibility to watch the smaller children more closely, and I wasn't allowed to go ice skating for a week. I thought my mother was being absolutely unfair and I was terribly angry. I remember how long it took me to get over my outrage and to enjoy my cousins' company again.

But most Friday evenings it was just Mamma, Papa and me, and I got to sit in the dining room where I was treated like a grown-up. Amid the clatter of eating and drinking, we talked about the week: what I had done at school; what news the workers had brought my mother; whom my father had hired to work on the farm; which animals were sick or about to give birth. I was included in every part of every discussion.

After supper, when the dishes had been washed, my job was to put everything away. The china, silverware and glasses were carefully returned to the dresser for safe keeping. Then we moved to the sitting room for the next stage in our ritual.

"Gabi, get the chessboard from the dresser," Papa said. "It's time for our rematch. And don't think you're going to beat me this week either!"

There in the back of the dresser, behind the dishes, behind the photo albums, was the chess set. It was a beautiful wooden set that my father had received as a child. The pieces were handcarved and looked like real kings, queens and knights. The knights carried shields and spears and sat on little horses with bulging eyes and pricked-up ears. My father had taught me to play when I was quite young. I was a good player, and careful of every move, but never good enough to beat him. I'm not sure our rabbi would have necessarily approved of our playing chess on the sabbath. This was meant to be a time of prayer and quiet reflection. But it was our tradition, and we would not have given it up for anything in the world. There in the comfort of the sitting room, with my mother reading in the big armchair by the window, our conversations continued late into the night.

This was my life as a child, and until I was almost eleven years old it was mostly filled with good times and happy memories. But it was there in our sitting room, one Friday evening, that we first talked of the disturbing events that were already beginning to change our lives.

"Papa," I said that evening, "do you remember a boy in my class called Martin? Well, he said the strangest thing today. He said that pretty soon I won't be able to go to school any more because I'm a Jew."

My father's hand stopped in the middle of a chess

move as he glanced at my mother. She stopped reading and rested the book on her lap.

"What was he talking about?" I asked.

My father fumbled with a chess piece. As he adjusted his glasses I noticed a slight trembling in his hands. "There is talk, Gabi," he began uneasily. "Some things are happening in other countries."

"What kind of things?"

"Well," Papa began, "let me try to explain. You know about the Nazi Party, the political party ruling Germany now, and about its leader, Adolf Hitler. And you know that the German army has already invaded Poland, Denmark, Norway and other countries."

I nodded. In school we had learned about the government in Germany, and about how Hitler's army was taking over much of Europe.

Papa continued. "Hitler and his Nazis despise the Jewish people. There have been reports in the papers about Jews in Germany being forced to give up their businesses. But it's hard to believe these rumours can be true. And it hasn't happened here in Czechoslovakia. I don't believe it has anything to do with us." His face was so serious that I suddenly felt worried.

"But, Papa, what if it has? Martin said that pretty soon

Jews won't even be able to stay in their homes. And he sounded so angry and nasty. They can't take away our houses, can they?"

"There, there, Gabilinka. You mustn't worry. Nothing terrible will happen to us. And you can tell this Martin that I said so. All right?"

I nodded, but my father's response had done little to reassure me. I thought of a conversation I had had earlier in the week, with Dora, a girl in my class. Mr. Reich had just returned our spelling tests. I was looking at my poor results and worrying about what my parents would think when Dora came up behind me and said, quite matter-of-factly, "It's because you're Jewish."

"What?" I replied, confused.

"You did so badly on the test because you're Jewish." Dora went on to explain that her parents had told her that Jews weren't very smart. It was something about Jews having smaller brains, so that we couldn't understand things as well as other people. I was astounded by what she was saying. Surely this was a joke, and any minute Dora would burst into laughter! But she spoke with assurance, as if she was certain every word she was saying was true. Somehow, I felt that I couldn't even begin to tell my parents about that conversation.

"Gabi, I think this chess game will have to continue next week," Papa said, interrupting my thoughts. "Put the board back in the dresser and get ready for bed. I will be up shortly to kiss you goodnight."

As I walked to the dining room with the chessboard, I overheard my mother talking.

"I got a letter from my sister in Germany today." Mamma sounded anxious but she spoke quietly. "She writes that Jews in Berlin are now forbidden to have cars, and they can't even use the tram any more! How are they supposed to do their errands, especially now that they can't shop at the same hours as other people. What next?"

"Listen," said Papa. "I know the newspaper reports don't sound good. I read an article some time ago about the synagogues in Germany being looted and ransacked one night. They're calling it *Kristallnacht* — the Night of Broken Glass. Thousands of Jews were rounded up, beaten, arrested or sent away. More and more reports like this are appearing. But we are a long way from Berlin, and from all these horrors. Besides, even if things change here, events like this won't affect us. We are good citizens with a strong business that many people rely on. We have plenty of friends. Do you think our neighbours would turn us away from their shops? People here would never allow harm to come to us. So stop worrying. Nothing will happen to us. And above all, we mustn't frighten Gabi with these stories."

I carefully replaced the chessboard in the dresser, and locked the doors and put the key back in the kitchen. As I slowly climbed the stairs to my room, I was baffled that, for the first time, my parents were excluding me from an important conversation. If they were keeping things from me, something serious must be happening. I thought about our sabbath and the traditions that never changed. Somehow, this Friday night felt different.

Chapter Four

I ENTERED MY BEDROOM and slumped on my bed, grabbing the china doll that rested on my pillow. Nina had given me the doll as a gift for one of my birthdays. Her porcelain face was hand painted in the softest shades of colour — pink for the lips and blue for the eyes — making her look almost lifelike. Her black hair glinted in the light, and her handmade party clothes were embroidered with silk thread. She was one of my most precious possessions.

Cradling my doll in my arms, I thought back over my conversation with my parents. It made no sense to me that bad things could be happening to Jews. But what I had told my mother and father about Martin and his angry warning to me was only the beginning. I had not told them about the other things happening at school.

Only yesterday, there had been a scene in the schoolyard. My friend Armin had been stopped by some boys and pushed down and punched so hard that there were bruises on his face today. Mr. Reich, who had come running outside to help Armin, was one of the few teachers who seemed to care about this hostility. When Dora told me I had done poorly on my spelling test because I was Jewish, it was Mr. Reich who interrupted her and told her she was talking nonsense. After Martin said that pretty soon I wouldn't be able to go to school, Mr. Reich kept him in after school for being disruptive. Most of the other teachers didn't seem bothered by the changing atmosphere, and some almost seemed to approve of it; they turned their backs and pretended nothing was wrong. I was puzzled and worried by all this. What was so wrong, these days, with being a Jew?

These thoughts swirled through my mind as I prepared for bed. I was so preoccupied with my thoughts that I did not even hear my father enter my room. "What stories are filling your head now, Gabi?" he asked as he sat heavily on the side of my bed, wiping a fine sheen of sweat from his brow. His breathing was difficult from the short climb up the stairs. When had climbing become so hard for him, I wondered briefly.

"Papa," I began slowly, trying hard to stay calm. "Please tell me the truth. I'm not a baby any more and I know when things aren't right. Even Nina has been acting strange lately, and she's my best friend! Just yesterday, she said her parents might not let her play at our house any more. None of this makes any sense to me."

"Gabilinka, believe me, it makes no sense to me either." For the first time I saw the confusion and sorrow in my father's eyes. I realized that he had been worrying about these changes more than he had let on. "Some people like to think they are stronger, smarter and better than we are," he said with a sigh. "And they blame the Jews for just about everything. They blame us when businesses fail, when others don't have enough to eat, even when their children do poorly in school!"

"But why blame us, Papa?" I asked. "What has it got to do with us?"

Papa sighed again. "It has absolutely nothing to do with us," he assured me. "But our people have often been wrongly blamed, Gabi. We are seen as being different, and when things go wrong it's easier for people to blame us than to look at their own responsibility. It's also easier for the government to pretend that everything is someone else's fault. In this case, the authorities in Germany are making Jews the scapegoat for poverty and unemployment."

"But, Papa, how can people believe that?"

"You know people in Germany have had some hard times," he reminded me. "When people are feeling desperate, they look for someone to blame. And they also look for an easy answer. Some people have convinced themselves that if they can only get rid of us, all their problems will disappear. You and I know this is nonsense, but some people will believe anything that makes them feel better. They are the ones causing us all of these problems. And unfortunately, they are convincing others to believe this nonsense as well."

I understood what my father was saying to me, and I felt very grown up to be talked to this way. But it didn't help my worries. Slowly I began to tell him the things that had been happening at school — my spelling test, and Dora, and how Armin had been knocked down. I told him about all my Jewish friends being teased and bullied. When I thought of all these things together, it seemed that my whole world was out of control.

"Papa, I'm scared," I said softly, and tears gathered in my eyes and streamed down my face. I was frightened — frightened of what was happening to my friends and happening to our family in Germany. I was afraid that awful things might soon happen to us. I cried and cried, letting my fears pour out of me.

"Gabi, listen carefully," my father said firmly, cupping my tear-stained face in his hands. "There is something you must always remember. Your mamma and I love you very much. We are here to protect you and keep you safe."

I hugged him as tight as I could.

"Remember the time you fell off your bicycle and you were nearly hit by that car?" he asked. "Remember how I galloped out in front of that car, waving my arms like a windmill and bellowing for the driver to stop."

For the first time since climbing into my bed, I laughed. "I was so scared you were going to get run over, I almost forgot I couldn't move my own leg!" I said. "Mamma thought we were both going to end up in the hospital."

"Well, the driver did stop and, aside from your sprained ankle, nothing serious happened. And I believe that, as long as we are brave and strong, we will be safe now."

"Papa, what if something bad starts to happen to me? What if someone tries to attack me? What do I do?" I asked.

"Gabi, I will fight with my last breath to make sure no harm comes to you." Papa spoke with such certainty that, for the first time since coming up to my room, I took an easy breath. I hugged him again.

"I learned a new piano piece this week, Papa. I want to play it for you in the morning."

"Sleep tight, my Gabilinka." My father held me close and whispered in my ear the words that were my night-time lullaby:

I will shelter you from harm,
You must have no fear,
You'll be safe, my precious child,
You'll be safe, my dear.

There in my father's arms, I believed that everything would be all right. I knew that my papa loved me, and I felt hopeful that I would always be safe, no matter what.

Chapter Five

IT'S HARD TO SAY exactly when I knew that things weren't going to get better. For the next few months I pretended that nothing important was changing. But deep down, I knew I was lying to myself. Everything was changing.

At school, there were more and more incidents of my Jewish friends being bullied. Sometimes I tried to help, if one of my friends was being hounded. But this was dangerous. There were so many of them and so few of us. It was better just to walk by with your head down and hope that you wouldn't be the next target.

It was also becoming harder and harder to talk to some of the kids. When I told Dora about my friends being picked on, she said they must have done something to deserve it. When I showed Nettie the broken window glass outside Mrs. Springer's bakery, she denied that being Jewish had anything to do with it. Even Nina was beginning to pull away from me.

When it was just the two of us together, nothing was different. We laughed, held hands and shared stories as always. But I began to notice that whenever Nina's brother appeared on the scene, Nina would become withdrawn and distant. If her parents were around, she would avoid me altogether. One morning, as I was hurrying to get ready for school, I looked out the window and saw Nina and her brother walking quickly by our driveway. For years Nina had stopped and waited for me there. But that morning, as she slowed in front of my house, her brother pulled her by the arm and she didn't stop. After school, she hurried out the door to walk home with someone else. I knew our friendship was in trouble, but I couldn't believe she would act this way.

One day I came right out and confronted her. At first she denied there was anything wrong, but finally she confessed that her parents were becoming more and more anxious about our friendship. They had read the newspaper articles listing restrictions against Jews in other countries. They knew about the beatings in town, and the nighttime attacks on Jewish storekeepers. They were worried that their daughter's friendship with a Jewish girl might cause trouble for them.

"It's not that I want to stop being your friend, it's just that my parents think it might be better if we didn't see so much of each other." Nina could not quite look me in the eye as she struggled to explain the situation. "My brother is the worst of all," she continued. "He's hanging out with this group of boys who think the attacks on Jews are just what the country needs. They're talking about joining the army so they can all wear uniforms and carry guns. Then they'll really be dangerous."

I was so stunned that I couldn't reply. "Gabi," Nina added, taking my hand, "I'm so mixed up, I'm not sure what to do. But for now I can't go against my parents. Maybe all this will be over soon, and we can go back to the way things were." She didn't sound the least bit convincing.

Then one day the most disturbing thing of all happened at school. Mr. Reich mysteriously disappeared. We all arrived as usual that morning, walked into the class and sat down, waiting for him to arrive. We were wondering why he was late when suddenly a strange man came into the classroom. He walked stiffly and awkwardly to the front and turned to face us.

"Class, your old teacher will not be coming back. Starting today, I will be your instructor. My name is Mr.

Cherny. You will stand when you address me."

Mr. Cherny was tall and somewhat stern-looking, not at all like Mr. Reich. He had an annoying sniffle that punctuated his sentences, and he dabbed ceaselessly at his nose. He never looked directly at us, but instead bent over his desk to take attendance and to assign work. He didn't appear to want to be here any more than we wanted him! As for me, I was shocked. This new teacher hadn't even explained to us where Mr. Reich had gone. Why was Mr. Cherny avoiding eye contact, as if he knew something he didn't want to tell us.

No one said a word as we got out our textbooks and began to work. Partway through the afternoon I finally mustered my courage to ask the question we'd all been thinking. Cautiously I raised my hand and stood as Mr. Cherny pointed to me.

"Excuse me, Mr. Cherny," I said, keeping my eyes lowered slightly, "could you please tell us where Mr. Reich is?"

He frowned. "Why are you asking me? I don't know anything more about it than you do. I was told to report to class, and I do as I'm told. It's not my fault he's gone. Lots of people like Mr. Reich are gone. Haven't you noticed?" Mr. Cherny scrubbed his nose frantically with a large handkerchief as I sat down and hid my burning face in my geography book.

I was more confused than ever. What did he mean by "people like Mr. Reich"? What was so different about Mr. Reich? It was then that it first occurred to me that Mr. Reich was Jewish. Had he been sent away because of that? If he had been sent away because he was Jewish, would others be sent away too? Would my family be sent away?

That day, I walked home from school alone. Nina had again run out the door without me and I didn't feel like having the company of my other friends. I needed to think again about what was happening and why. When I arrived home, Papa was sitting in the kitchen, having tea by himself. I slumped into the seat beside him, put my head down and poured out the story of Mr. Reich's disappearance.

"I have no idea where he's gone, Papa. I don't know if he's gone for good, or if he'll be back. The other teacher looked kind of embarrassed about the whole thing, but he didn't seem to know anything about where Mr. Reich was either. What's going to happen next?" I looked up at Papa's face, searching for the answers that no one seemed to have. Papa looked pale and tired.

"Papa, are you okay?" I suddenly realized that it was

the middle of the afternoon. He was never home at this time. "Did something happen? Where's Mamma?"

"Mamma is fine, Gabi. She's gone to get some medicine for me. It's nothing serious, just the usual small pain here," he said, pointing to his chest. His face twisted slightly and then relaxed as the spasm passed. "Gabi, make me some more tea, please," he whispered, removing his glasses and slowly rubbing his eyes. "I'm fine, Gabilinka," he insisted as he looked up and saw the worry in my face. "Really, I'm fine," he repeated, more firmly.

I rose from the table and put the kettle on the stove, dumped out the teapot and put in fresh tea. It wasn't the first time that Papa had needed medicine for the pain in his chest. I had known for some time that he wasn't well. But, like so many other things, I tried to pretend that his illness wasn't serious. Maybe I was ignoring what was happening before my eyes. Papa did seem more tired lately. At night, he would fall asleep in his big armchair as soon as supper was over. Mamma had to wake him and help him up the stairs to bed. And lately, when Papa and I went on walks together, he needed to stop and rest. Often he would reach into his pocket for a pill to ease the pain in his chest.

The door creaked behind me and I looked up to see

Mamma coming in with a package in her hands. She kissed me softly on the forehead before approaching Papa and setting a bottle of pills before him. I poured hot water into the teapot and brought it to Papa with a mug. Wearily he poured his tea and picked up the medicine.

"I'm going to lie down for a few minutes. Call me when supper is ready." He rose slowly from the table and smiled a reassuring smile at my mother and me. "I'm lucky to have a family that takes such good care of me," he said as he walked out of the kitchen.

Mamma sighed deeply after he left. "Come on, Gabi, start peeling the potatoes for supper."

"Mamma, I have to tell you what happened at school today," I said, moving towards the pantry.

"Yes, darling ... I think two potatoes will be enough tonight, don't you? I'm not sure how much your papa will eat."

"Mamma," I began again, and then stopped. She wasn't listening.

There was so much I wanted to tell her about my day at school. I needed to talk to her about Mr. Reich leaving, and the teacher who was there to take his place. I needed to talk about Nina's reaction to all the trouble. I needed help understanding what was happening around me. And

I needed to talk about Papa and his illness. But I knew this was not the time. Mamma looked too worried for me to trouble her. For now, I would have to keep my thoughts to myself and work things out on my own.

Chapter Six

APRIL 1941

SIX MONTHS LATER, my papa died. I felt as if my world had collapsed. Though I had known he wasn't well, I was completely unprepared for his death. Surely he couldn't have been that sick. And yet, in the months after Mr. Reich's disappearance, I had watched Papa become weaker and weaker.

Eventually, instead of waiting by the door for him to come back from work each day, I would return home from school and rush to his bedroom, where he spent most of his time. He looked pathetically pale and sickly lying in his bed.

"Papa, won't you please try to get up today?" I would beg as I knelt by his bed and held his hand. "Maybe we could play a game of chess. I know I can beat you, for sure. Open your eyes and get out of bed."

My mother would whisper for me to be quiet. "Can't you see that Papa is resting? Run along, Gabi, and don't tire your father." Stories and merriment no longer filled each room in our house. As Papa became more ill, our home grew hushed. But I couldn't believe it was serious — couldn't let myself believe. Not when so many other things were going wrong in my life. Papa *had* to get better.

Then, in the middle of one night, my mother sent for the doctor, and I knew things must be very bad. Still I pretended nothing was happening. I hid in my room, and I held my pillow tightly over my head as the sound of my mother's cries came through my bedroom door. Hours passed, and then Mamma came into my room to tell me Papa had died. I tried not to believe her, but I knew it was true.

We held each other through the night and I cried until I felt I had cried out every tear in my body. By morning the house was filled with family and friends, comforting my mother and me, cooking and helping prepare things for the funeral. Aunts, neighbours and friends all tried to get me to eat.

"Gabi — come, dear, you must have a bite."

"Gabi, you'll be sick if you don't eat something."

"Gabi, just a few bites to keep up your strength."

"Leave me alone!" I screamed. "I'm not a baby! Get out of my way!" I ran from the house to the barn, where I sat alone in the hayloft. I was angry that Papa had died, and sad and worried. How were we going to manage the farm without Papa there to take care of things? What would happen to us without him? It wasn't fair that he had died, and I couldn't imagine our lives without his strong and caring presence.

"I miss him so much," I cried one Friday night to my mother. I was setting the table for sabbath and as I knelt in front of the dresser to get out the dishes I needed, I saw the chessboard. It rested untouched in the back of the dresser, a reminder of how things had changed. Not only had Papa died, but it seemed as if everything else in my home and my village was changing as well.

Lately it was just Mamma and me on Friday nights. My aunts, uncles and cousins could no longer join us because Jews were not permitted to stay out at night beyond a certain time. Our sabbath evenings together were quiet, for we had little to say to one another. Usually we sat in silence, each of us thinking about our own personal sadness. I watched Mamma carefully during those times. Was she as worried as I was?

Soon, more and more disturbing events began to happen in our village. We already knew from newspaper and radio reports that Czechoslovakia had been divided up and parts of the country in the west were now under Nazi rule. While our area was still independent, the attitudes towards Jews and the rules against them had spread throughout the country. One day, a notice appeared in town stating that all businesses owned by Jews would be run by "national supervisors." Jews could stay on and do the work, but they could no longer sign legal papers or control money. Some of these supervisors loved their new positions of power and showed disrespect and even ridicule for the former owners. We were lucky; the supervisor who appeared at our door one morning was a decent man. He looked uncomfortable with his position of authority, as if he didn't necessarily approve of what the government was doing. Still, to Mamma it felt as though the farm she and Papa had worked so hard to build was slowly slipping away.

To make matters worse, the workers on our farm began to leave, one by one. Some said goodbye and tearfully apologized for the laws that now forbade them to work for Jews. Others simply stopped arriving for work. My mother tried her best to carry on managing both the farm and our home, and I helped as much as I could. But it was becoming impossible for us to do everything.

On top of that, some shopkeepers were beginning to

refuse to sell anything to Jews. While we were still able to shop in stores owned by our Jewish friends, they were having difficulty keeping their shelves stocked. Food and other products were all being sent to the army, creating real shortages for civilians. Coffee and tea had completely disappeared. We made a sort of tea by brewing leaves from the linden trees that grew on our property. It didn't smell like the tea we'd known, but it was hot and quite good. Meat, milk and vegetables were still plentiful on our farm, but flour, sugar and other necessary items were harder and harder to come by.

By now, I was attending a school for Jewish children only. I didn't mind the school very much, because I knew most of the other students and many of the teachers. My friend Marishka was there, and so were Nettie, Ruthie and others. Even Mr. Reich was a teacher at this school, and it was wonderful to be reunited with him. Still, I missed my old friends. Sometimes I would catch a glimpse of Nina walking to our old school or shopping with her new friends. If my eyes happened to meet hers, or if I waved to her, she would quickly turn away, as if she had been caught doing something terrible.

How could this have happened? One minute we had been like sisters, sharing our most important secrets. The next minute it seemed we hardly knew one another. At times I felt I hated her for deserting me, but then, I would feel sorry for her. She too must be frightened these days. To be caught being friendly to a Jew was dangerous. Her home might be raided, or someone in her family might be attacked.

Walks to and from school were no longer filled with pleasure and fun. My friends and I walked quickly, with our heads down. We were careful to avoid the bullies who loved to single out Jewish children — or, worse, the new units of soldiers who had begun to appear in town. They were members of the Slovak People's Party, a Slovak version of the Nazi party that was in power in Germany. They wore stiff black uniforms with tall black boots, and they carried rifles on their shoulders. They had harsh, hostile faces. Some of the younger ones were the brothers of children I had gone to school with. But whether or not you knew them didn't matter. If you were picked out by one of these men, you could be beaten or arrested.

One day when I was on my way to school, Nina slipped a note into my pocket. Finally, I thought, she's trying to make contact with me. I was wrong. The note read: "Don't speak to me again. I'm sorry, but I can't be your friend!"

It seemed that everything in my life was slipping away. First, Papa had died. Then all those horrible laws against Jews had been passed. And now my friends were deserting me.

I got that note from Nina on the same day that the letter arrived stating that we had to wear a yellow star on our clothing, so that everyone could see that we were Jews. At first I told my mother that I would never obey this rule. I would fight anyone who dared tell me what to wear. But, as with everything else, we eventually gave in. I think we tried to convince ourselves that, maybe if we just did this one thing, nothing more would happen. I watched my mother sew a yellow star on every dress, blouse, sweater and coat I owned.

"This is a horrible time for all of us," she said. "I'm sure we won't have to do this for long. But for now, we must do as we're told." Her sad face did little to ease my fears.

If only my father were here, I thought. I was certain he would have made things better. Papa had said everything would be fine as long as we were together. Well, we weren't together any more. I knew I still had to be brave and strong, but that was hard when so many awful things were happening. Our village just wasn't the same, and I didn't feel the same in it. I felt like an outsider, an outcast. We could barely leave our house any more except to go to school. Besides, if we did go outside, there was nowhere to go. Stores and even neighbours turned us away. It reminded me of something Papa had said that time when he thought I wasn't listening. He had told Mamma that our neighbours would never turn their backs on us. Well, he had been wrong.

Sometimes, at night, I lay in bed and cried softly into my pillow, so Mamma wouldn't hear. I thought about Papa at those times, and what he might have said to comfort me.

"Gabilinka, do not be afraid. Take care of your Mamma. And remember, I'm watching out for you."

Remembering Papa was like having him close to me. It made me feel better. If I could keep on thinking about him and remembering him, I would have the courage to face anything.

Chapter Seven

JANUARY 1942

IN THE MONTHS FOLLOWING Papa's death, Mamma and I slowly returned to our regular routine. At first, when I went back to school, my friends went out of their way to be nice to me. They sat with me at lunch and made sure we did the things I wanted to do. The teachers gave me only a small amount of homework. Even the boys were unusually kind.

On my second day back, one of the boys in my class offered to carry my books home from school. His name was Jeremy, and for some time I had secretly liked him. As we walked home together Jeremy entertained me with funny stories about Mr. Reich and the things he had done and said in class during the week I was away. The stories made me laugh out loud. The next day at school, Jeremy kept glancing in my direction and smiling so much that Mr. Reich finally had to ask him why he looked so happy. My face went red with embarrassment as everyone giggled.

Aside from Jeremy's attention, Marishka brought me sweets that her mother had baked. I have no idea how she managed to find the ingredients to make some of my favourite treats. But every day, for weeks, Marishka brought me something special: a cupcake, a cookie, and one day even a piece of chocolate. Maybe she thought this would somehow fill up the empty place in my heart.

At first, I felt awkward and self-conscious about all the attention. But then I remembered doing exactly the same thing when Marishka's grandmother died. I hadn't known how to tell Marishka how sorry I was that she had lost her grandmother. So instead I had brought her things from home that I thought would make her feel better: a flower, some notepaper, a hairband.

In the end I was grateful for everyone's concern and thoughtfulness. It did help to have my friends taking care of me. But sometimes I wondered if Nina knew about Papa dying. Our village was so small that the news of anyone's death always spread quickly. When we were best friends, Nina and I had always turned to each other when things went wrong. These days I wondered if she even cared about what was happening to me and the others. I tried to push the thoughts of Nina out of my head. As far as I knew, Nina was gone from my life. It didn't help to think about her. I had to get on with my life, and that meant concentrating on school, my friends and my home.

News reports about the war were coming fast and furious these days. And most of the time they were discouraging. Country after country was falling to the advancing German soldiers. Men and boys in our village and neighbouring towns had left to join them, leaving the women to carry on with businesses. Rallies proclaiming Germany's conquests were held in the larger cities. When one of those demonstrations occurred, we were very careful to stay indoors. Local residents, filled with a sense of victory were even quicker to come after Jews.

On the last Sunday of every month, Mamma and I cleaned out the dresser. Each dish, glass and piece of silver was carefully removed from the dresser, dusted and polished, and tenderly replaced. My mother handled each item as lovingly as a newborn child. When the dresser had been emptied of all of its contents, we cleaned it inside and out. We rubbed and polished the doors and shelves until they shone with a deep, reddish glow. We both knew it was silly to take so much time each week cleaning things we hardly ever used. But it felt good to do it. It reminded us of happier times. We were there one Sunday, cleaning out the dresser, when we heard the doorbell ring.

"Gabi, look first, before you open the door," Mamma cautioned me.

I ran to the front window and looked outside. Lately, the streets were always quiet. Gasoline was strictly rationed and cars and trucks were rarely driven except in emergencies. "It's Marishka's mother, Mamma. Maybe she has another cake for us." But as I opened the door, I saw that this time there was no cake. Marishka's mother looked anxious, and she kept glancing over her shoulder as if she thought someone might be following her.

"Gabi, I need to speak to your mother," she said urgently.

"Come in, come in," my mother said, appearing at my side. "Gabi, go make some tea."

"No, no tea," Marishka's mother said. "I have very little time, and we have to talk."

We settled together in the sitting room as our visitor untied her shawl. Her face was flushed and tired. It was a few moments before she could begin to talk.

"There are new rumours," she said. "Nothing for certain yet. But I had a note from my sister. You remember, the one who lives in Levocha. She managed to get a message to me by a friend who was travelling this way. It seems that in Levocha there have been raids by the soldiers. People are being put on trucks and taken away."

"Raids!" I cried. There had been nothing like this in our village. A few homes had been looted, and furniture and other belongings destroyed. Some people had been beaten in the streets because they were defying the laws by breaking curfew, travelling without a permit or not wearing their stars prominently enough. But never before had we heard of anyone being taken away. "What do you mean, they were taken away? Taken where? And who was taken?"

Marishka's mother looked in my direction, and then back at Mamma. "I'm not sure if Gabi should be hearing this. It frightens Marishka so much that I've stopped telling her things."

"Gabi can hear," my mother replied grimly. "There are only the two of us now. I will not keep things from her."

"All right," agreed Marishka's mother, but she clearly wasn't persuaded. "My sister wrote that at first the young men were taken, those who hadn't followed the regulations set by the government. Next, the poorest Jews were taken, then old people, and —" she paused, "young girls, Gabi's and Marishka's age and older. The girls were taken from their families, herded onto trucks and driven out of town."

"God help us!" my mother cried. "Where have they taken them, and what do they want with young girls?"

"They say it's for work. The girls are strong and they're

needed in factories. They say they'll be back in a few weeks. But we don't know where they've gone."

Her voice trailed off and the three of us sat in silence. My mind raced. I knew some girls my age in Levocha. Had they been dragged from their homes? And what about me and my friends? Were we also in danger? Levocha wasn't all that far away. It was one thing to wear stars and switch schools. But the thought of being forced to leave home was almost too much for me. I hardly noticed Marishka's mother standing up and moving towards the door.

"I'd better go now. I have been away long enough, and my family will worry. God bless you both. Be well and stay strong." Mamma closed the door behind her and we watched through the window as she walked quickly down the street.

I was in a daze, with confusing thoughts swirling through my head. Mamma's face looked worn and weary as she turned to face me.

"Gabi, it's time to make plans for your safety," she began.

"Mamma, it's not just my safety we need to worry about. It's *our* safety."

"Yes, but you heard Marishka's mother. I know you won't want to hear this, but I've been thinking. You remember the Kos family, who used to work on our farm? They live up in the mountains now. They are Christians, but they are good people. When they stopped working here, they said that if there was ever some way they could help, we only had to ask. They loved your papa very much and they're not afraid of what might happen to them if they help Jews. I think you should go and stay with them. You will be safer there."

"Go away? Mamma, how can you even think of such a thing?" I was so horrified I could barely speak.

"Don't look at me that way, Gabi. It will only be for a short time, until all this trouble passes."

"Mamma, I won't go!" I shouted. "Please, please don't send me away! How could I leave you? How can you think of separating us?"

My mother turned her head away so she didn't have to watch the tears streaming down my cheeks. All I could think about was what my papa had said to me at night: we would be safe as long as we were together. How could I possibly be brave and strong when Papa had left me and now Mamma was threatening to do the same? No! Under no circumstances would I leave without my mother.

"I don't know what else to do to keep you safe, Gabilinka," Mamma whispered. "If the soldiers come looking for you, there is nowhere here for you to hide."

"I'm safest with you, Mamma. I'm sure of it. And there are plenty of places I could hide in this house," I said, desperately looking around. "I could hide in a closet, or in the basement, or even in the dresser."

"The dresser?" She looked doubtful.

"Of course. What better hiding place? We could take out the shelf in the middle to make room for me. There's even a lock. No one would ever think of looking in there." I knew I was grasping at straws, but I had to have a plan. I was sure I'd be safe hiding in the dresser. Besides, I couldn't believe I'd ever need to. Not here, not in our home.

"The dresser," she said again. "We would have to take all the things out of there and put them safely away somewhere, to make room for you."

"Of course," I replied, hugging her. I knew I had won. I was sure I'd never have to hide in the dresser. What was important was that I wouldn't be sent away. I would stay here with Mamma. "We'll take everything out. We'll get it all ready. But promise me you won't send me away."

My mother hugged me back, tightly. "All right, Gabilinka, you win. You can stay here, but we'll prepare the dresser in case we need it. And I pray it will keep you safe."

Chapter Eight

APRIL 1942

SEVERAL MONTHS PASSED, and we seemed to forget about the conversation with Marishka's mother. I was far too busy thinking about other things. First of all, I had to concentrate on my schoolwork. Then, each day after school, I had to go straight home to help Mamma on the farm. Feeding the cows and cleaning and raking the barn were now my responsibilities. All my spare time was taken up with these chores. I understood how important it was to make sure the cows were well taken care of. For now, we were still able to earn money by selling milk to the kosher dairy, where it was prepared under the watchful eye of the rabbi and according to strict religious rules. But we didn't know how long this would last.

The fields were left untended. It was impossible for us to manage all the land on our own. But Mamma kept a small garden that provided us with fresh vegetables. Each night I fell into bed exhausted. It felt like only minutes before Mamma was shaking me awake the next morning, when everything would begin again.

One day, as I was helping Mamma clean the house, there was a quiet knock at the back door. I ran to answer it, first checking out the window to see who was there. A man and woman stood huddled together, two young children at their sides. The man glanced nervously over his shoulder as the woman tapped on the door. I opened it, thinking at first that they were drifters looking for a handout. Gypsies often travelled through the region, selling housewares, scraps of material and even homemade herbal remedies. In the past, we had usually given them food as well as buying their wares. But as soon as the door was open, I realized that these were not gypsies. They were shabbily dressed and looked as if they hadn't slept in days.

"We saw the mezuzah on your door." The man spoke softly, and pointed to the religious emblem fixed to our doorpost. His Slovak was interspersed with Polish words I struggled to understand. "We are also Jews. Will you give us something to eat? We've been travelling a long time and the children are so hungry." He looked down at the boy and girl beside him, their tired eyes wide with hope.

Mamma appeared at my side, quickly ushered the family into our kitchen and sat them down. As we shared with them what little food we had, their story unfolded. They had come from Poland, hiding in barns by day and travelling through the woods by night. They were heading west, to Ukraine, where other family members lived.

"What are things like now in Poland?" asked Mamma. She had cousins there and had not had a letter from them in many months.

"They're not good," the man replied through a mouthful of bread and cheese. "The Jews who are left have been moved to ghettos — sections of the cities restricted only to Jews. There is little food there, and conditions are terrible. People live there like prisoners in their own towns.

"The Nazis are everywhere. You can't escape them. Each day, trucks appear in the streets. The soldiers go house to house, rounding up Jewish families and moving them to the train stations. Resistance is impossible. And what's worse, the local people stand on the sidewalks and watch, and do nothing. Some even shout encouragement to the Nazis."

"Where are the trains taking them?" I asked. The man glanced at his wife before responding. "We're told they're being relocated to other parts of the country where they'll be able to build new homes for themselves. But we know it's not true. Some of them are going to work camps — if they're lucky. But there are also stories of Jews ending up in other camps, where they're simply murdered. We were lucky to get out. You'd be best to leave as well. Who knows how long it will be before the same thing happens here?"

Silence hung in the air. The family quickly finished eating and, as darkness fell, they went on their way. Before they left, Mamma stuffed some extra vegetables and rolls into the woman's backpack.

"For the children," she whispered, as the stranger hugged her.

For days I thought about the family and the man's ominous warning. Marishka's mother had already told us about factories and work camps. But this was the first I'd heard about death camps. The thought filled me with fear, but also disbelief. Surely our people weren't being sent away to die! Mamma said nothing to me after the family's visit, and I couldn't bring myself to question her.

Marishka and I walked to school together everyday. Somehow it felt safer to walk with a friend. One morning, about a week after this family had stopped at our house, we were on our way to school as usual. To pass the time we played a game, pretending we were moving to a new country and could only take ten things from all of our belongings. I said I would take my doll, of course, as well as my picture album with the photographs of all our relatives. Marishka said she could never leave behind her locket, and the teddy bear she had been given as an infant. Its one eye was gone and her mother had patched the bear in many places over the years, but it was a treasured keepsake.

Our conversation stopped abruptly as we reached the school and realized that something was very wrong. The gate, which was usually wide open, was closed. A big metal chain with a heavy lock was wrapped around the fence. Inside, the playground and building were deserted. There were no teachers in sight.

Marishka and I approached the gate cautiously. Several of our friends were already there, gathered around a big sign hung over the fence. We joined the others and read the announcement:

JEWS ARE FORBIDDEN TO ATTEND SCHOOL.
THE BUILDING IS HEREBY CLOSED.

For several minutes we stood there as the news sank in. No more school! At first Marishka and I just looked at each other, not knowing what to do. I tugged hesitantly on the chain, perhaps hoping that if I pulled hard enough it might open in my hand. Our books, pencils and other belongings were inside. How could we get them back? What were we going to do all day if we couldn't go to school?

At any other time in our lives we would have been delighted that school was closed. But not now. Now we knew something serious had happened. This was yet one more rule separating us from everyone else. Our lives were being taken away, little by little, and we were becoming more and more frightened as each new law was passed.

The students began to move away, saying little to one another. Marishka and I joined arms, holding onto each other for comfort. We turned slowly from the building and began to walk home.

"Do you think we'll ever see Mr. Reich again?" I asked sadly.

"Oh, I'm sure we will," replied Marishka, though she didn't sound convinced.

We walked on in silence. Finally Marishka turned to me. "Let's look on the bright side," she said. "No more homework!"

I smiled a little and said. "And no more awful spelling tests!"

"No more long walks to school in the cold and rain!" she continued.

"And no more boring lectures!" Our pace quickened as we tried to cheer each other up.

"I'm going to sleep in every morning from now on," declared Marishka.

"Oh, no!" I groaned. "I'm going to have to work even harder on the farm. My back aches just thinking about it."

We were rounding a street corner and were so deeply involved in our conversation that we almost walked straight into the soldier who blocked our path. My heart nearly stopped as I looked up into his glowering face.

"Jews! Why don't you watch where you're going?" he barked, glaring at us.

"I ... I'm sorry, sir," I stammered. "We ... we didn't see ... we ... we didn't mean ..."

"What are you mumbling? Are you too stupid to answer a simple question?" He moved closer to us. Marishka and I were paralyzed with fear. My eyes moved from his shiny black boots up the length of his brown uniform and rested on his face. I gasped, realizing that I recognized him. His name was Ivan, and he was a friend of Nina's brother. He had been at Nina's house many times when I'd played there. He was quite young, only a few years older than me. But now, dressed in this uniform, he was like a different person.

"Did you hear me, Jew? Maybe I need to teach you a lesson about respect." He reached to his side and began to pull out a wooden stick swinging from his black belt. Marishka and I whimpered. What was he going to do? Was he going to beat us? Would he arrest us? I closed my eyes and covered my face with my hands as Marishka's fingers dug deeper into my arm.

"Ivan," a girl's voice chimed from across the street. "Ivan, how *are* you?"

My eyes opened a crack and I looked up. Ivan's arm was poised above my head, the stick swinging dangerously close to my face, but his face was turned towards the voice that had called him. I followed his gaze across the street and was astonished to see Nina waving and running towards us.

"Ivan, I haven't seen you for *ages*. I thought you were still away at school." Nina's face was flushed as she stopped in front of us. She didn't look once at Marishka and me, but kept her eyes focused on Ivan. "You look so much *older* in that uniform!" she gushed. Carefully she took his arm holding the stick and pulled it towards her.

"Nina? Nina! It's good to see you," said Ivan, momentarily distracted. "Where is your brother? Is he back from training yet?"

"Yes, yes, and he's been asking about you," Nina continued. Quietly but deliberately she moved to put herself between us and Ivan. "In fact, I think he may be at home now. Why don't you come with me? I'm out of school early because I have a doctor's appointment. If you come home with me, I'm sure my mother would love to feed you a *big* lunch." Nina chattered quickly, without pausing. Her voice was high and bright as she turned Ivan away from us.

"Aw, Nina. I'd love to come but I have these Jews to deal with." He pulled his arm from hers and turned to face us once more.

"Oh, why bother with them?" Nina asked, taking his arm again. "Come on. My mother was cooking this morning and the desserts should be ready by now. If we hurry they'll still be warm. When was the last time you had pancakes stuffed with your choice of cheese, jam, or poppyseed and honey?"

Ivan laughed and puffed out his chest. "I sure remember your mother's delicious food. And that really thick cream she used to make. Does she still make that?"

He turned again to snarl at Marishka and me. "You two, get out of here. And next time I catch you I won't let you off so easy."

I didn't know it then, but that would be the last time I ever saw Nina. In that moment our lives were separated for good. As Nina and Ivan reached the next corner, I saw her turn slightly, and our eyes met and said it all. I looked at her with gratitude and relief. She looked at me with friendship and pity.

Marishka tugged urgently on my arm and we ran in the opposite direction. We didn't stop running until we reached my home.

Chapter Nine

MARISHKA AND I burst through the front door, our faces white with fear. Mamma was startled to see us home from school so early and guessed instantly that something was wrong.

"What happened?" she cried. "You both look like you've seen a ghost."

It was several moments before Marishka and I could talk. Then the story came tumbling out of our mouths. We told Mamma how we had walked to school and found the school closed, we described the sign that said Jews could no longer attend, we told her about nearly bumping into the soldier. Mamma's face was tense with anger and fear as we described how we had thought we were going to be beaten or arrested even though the soldier was someone we knew. Finally we told her how Nina had saved us by luring the soldier away. By the time we finished recounting the whole story, we were exhausted.

"The first thing I'm going to do is go and tell Marishka's mother that Marishka is safe with us." Mamma spoke calmly and with authority. "I want you girls to stay in the sitting room while I'm gone, and open the door to no one. I'll be back in a few minutes."

We did as we were told, huddling together on the sitting-room couch. We didn't say a word to each other, but sat in silence, arms clasped, reliving the terror in our minds.

By the time Mamma returned home, we had calmed down. She fed us a big meal that we gobbled up in minutes. We hadn't realized how hungry we were until we sat down at the table. Then Mamma said Marishka could stay for the night. I think she realized how important it was for Marishka and me to be together, after everything we had shared that day.

Marishka's mother came over later in the day to see Marishka. The two of them stood in the hallway hugging each other for a long time. Once again Marishka and I described what had happened. They hugged again and cried with relief that everything had turned out well. I know Marishka's mother would have preferred to have her daughter home with her that evening, but seeing the looks on our faces, she agreed that Marishka could stay. Mamma helped us make up the extra bed in my room.

That night, Marishka and I lay in bed a long time, talking about the close call.

"Why do you think she did it?" Marishka asked at one point.

"Who did what?" I replied, puzzled.

"Nina. Why do you think she saved us? If she hadn't been there, I don't know what might have happened!"

The same question had been running through my head all day. Why, all of sudden, had Nina helped us? For months she had been avoiding me, obeying her parents by turning her back on our friendship. What had suddenly made her stand up for me? Why had she put herself at risk? It was hard to figure out.

"You know," I began, "I had finally convinced myself to stop thinking about Nina, to stop wanting her still to be my friend. I thought she didn't like me anymore. Now I'm more confused than ever."

"Well, I guess she still thinks about you," Marishka said. "Do you know how dangerous it was for her to interfere like that? If the soldier had figured out what she was doing, who knows what he might have done, to us and to Nina."

"I guess deep down she still sees me as her friend." I thought of all the years Nina and I had been friends, and how strong that friendship had been; how we had stood up for each other, trusted each other and been loyal to each other. Loyalty. The word meant so much. Like not turning your back on a friend when that friend was in trouble. Like being there to help when somebody needed you. Today Nina had shown me that she was still a loyal friend, that the pact between us still mattered to her.

"You two were pretty close," said Marishka.

I nodded and gulped. "Like sisters."

"Do you think, when all this is over, you can go back to being best friends like before?"

How could I answer that? It was hard to think any of this would ever be over. Each day we tried to tell ourselves that things were going to get better. And each day things seemed to get worse.

"What's going to happen to us?" Marishka asked, as if reading my thoughts. "You know, not just you and me and our families, but all the Jewish families?"

I didn't answer.

"You know," she continued, "lots of people are leaving the village. Haven't you noticed? Dora and her family, Armin and his parents, the Bottensteins, the Wohls. One day they're here and the next day they're gone. Other people are leaving too. I don't even know where they're going."

Still I didn't answer. I knew about people leaving our village. Just days earlier, Jeremy had walked by our house and stopped to tell me that he and his family were going to Palestine. They were leaving the following week. It would be terribly difficult and risky. His parents had paid someone a lot of money to get the exit papers, and to smuggle them out of the country in a truck. They would head first for the Baltic Sea, where they would cross into Palestine by boat. Despite the danger, they were determined to flee. Would they get there safely?

I hadn't seen much of Jeremy since our school had closed, but I often thought about him. After Papa died and Jeremy paid all that attention to me, he and I became special friends. He sometimes carried my books when we walked to school, and he often waited after class to walk me home. With all the dangers to Jews on the streets, I did feel safer when Jeremy was around. Now I had no idea if I'd ever see him again, and the thought saddened me. Standing in front of me, telling me that he was going away, he had looked so awkward and embarrassed. Finally, after a long silence, he had grabbed my hand and shaken it furiously, promised to write and run off before I could say a word.

I had also heard Marishka's mother saying something to Mamma about leaving. When I had asked Mamma about it, she had confessed that it was something she too had thought about. We had family in England, Switzerland and even America. Surely it would be safer to go to them. And yet, as we talked about the possibilities, we knew we couldn't bring ourselves to go. Somehow, leaving our home was scarier than staying and facing whatever difficulties might come up. Our home was here. Papa was buried here. How could we possibly go?

"I don't want to talk any more, Gabi," Marishka said, yawning loudly. "I'm so tired. I need to sleep." Within minutes her breathing had become slow and even, and I knew she was asleep.

For me it was a different matter. I lay awake for what seemed like hours, my mind racing over and over the events of the day. In my mind's eye I could still see the soldier's stick swinging over my head. I could feel my heart race in terror as his cruel and angry voice shouted at me. I could hear Nina's voice interrupting his hateful bullying. I kept telling myself to calm down and breathe deeply. I was safe, for now. And I had to keep my wits about me if I was going to stay that way.

And then I thought about Papa. When I was a child I used to have nightmares and he was the one who came to my bed to comfort me. His soothing voice always worked magic, and my nightmares would evaporate into nothing.

In the midst of those bad dreams, he always held me close and whispered his special lullaby in my ear:

I will shelter you from harm,
You must have no fear,
You'll be safe, my precious child,
You'll be safe, my dear.

Thinking about Papa helped me as I lay there in bed that night. Everything that had happened that day was like a bad dream. "Gabilinka," Papa would have said, "don't be frightened any more. I'm here now." I repeated Papa's poem over and over in my head, and eventually its soothing promises lulled me to sleep.

Chapter Ten

IN THE FOLLOWING MONTHS I found myself growing more and more careful about everything I did. In a way, it was a relief not to have to go to school. It meant I didn't have to walk through the streets of the town and risk another confrontation with a soldier. Even going to and from Marishka's house frightened me more than I had ever thought possible. I walked quickly, looking in all directions. At the first glimpse of a stranger in the distance, I would run at full speed for home, not lingering to see if the person was a friend or a possible foe. I preferred to have Marishka come to my house, but she was as frightened of the trip as I was, so most of the time I stayed at home with Mamma, helping her on the farm and in the house.

Day by day we heard more about the war. Mamma had managed to get hold of a radio from a former farm worker, even though Jews were forbidden to own radios.

At night, with all the lights out, we would try to tune in to news reports from other countries.

One year earlier the Soviet Union had entered the war against Germany, and soon after, the United States had joined the Allies too. These were huge countries. Surely, with so many people fighting the German side, the tide of the war would turn soon. Surely the conflict would soon be over. But month after month, the war continued, and the radio reports from German-controlled countries praised Hitler endlessly and promised that the Nazis would take over the whole world.

One morning, as I rolled over in bed, I realized that sunlight was already pouring in my bedroom window. It was late, way past daybreak. Why hadn't Mamma come in to wake me? I stared for a moment out the window. I couldn't remember when I had last taken the time to look at this wonderful view. The mountains were as beautiful as ever, covered in places by a thick blanket of fog, and scattered with green shrubs and blue shadows. It amazed me to think that, while so much of my world had changed dramatically, the mountains were the same as they had always been: as solid and dependable as the four walls of my room.

My door opened slowly and the creak of the hinge

pulled me back to the present. My mother's smiling face peered around the corner.

"Mamma? Is everything all right?" I asked. "You didn't wake me up."

"Happy birthday, Gabilinka," she cried, as she walked into my room holding a brightly wrapped parcel. "No, I didn't wake you today. As a special birthday treat, I let you sleep in as long as you wanted."

My birthday! I had practically forgotten that today was my birthday. I was astounded! My birthday had always been the most anticipated day of the year for me. One birthday was barely over when I began to look forward to the next. And here I was, forgetting all about it.

"It's not much of a gift this year, my darling," my mother said apologetically. I slowly unwrapped the colourful parcel and pulled out a hand-knitted scarf and matching mittens. Mamma had used every scrap of coloured yarn she had to create a woolly blend of shades and tones. I buried my face in the softness.

"They're beautiful, Mamma," I said, and I couldn't help seeing the look of relief in her eyes. "Just what I needed too."

"And now, Gabi, get up and dress quickly. Marishka and her mother are coming over to celebrate, along with a few of your old classmates. How would it look if you were late for your own party?"

My birthday lunch was a wonderful treat. Mamma had somehow managed to scrounge up some food we hadn't had for ages. There was cold soup with fresh cherries and dumplings filled with plums. There was even cinnamon and chocolate sprinkled over the birthday cake; thirteen candles and one for good luck. I blew them all out as my friends sang "Happy Birthday." Then I opened my gifts. One of my friends had brought a fascinating book about the seaside. She knew how much I missed the library at school. I had already read and reread every book we owned at home. Another friend brought material that Mamma said she would sew into a new skirt. I hadn't had any new clothes for a long time.

The best gift was from Marishka. She made me close my eyes as she placed a warm, furry bundle in my out-stretched arms.

"A kitten!" I cried. "Oh, Marishka, she's beautiful! Thank you so much!" I gave Marishka a quick hug as she explained that their cat had recently had kittens. Marishka had picked out this female for me and she was adorable. Irregular spots of black covered her otherwise white body. Even her eyes were unusual, one surrounded with a patch of black and the other ringed with pure white. Her paws were black, making her look as if she were wearing slippers. She was tiny, barely filling my hands, and she made the most pathetic sound as she opened her mouth to mew. It was hardly more than a squeak. I loved her immediately, and gathered the squirming kitten close to my face so I could nuzzle her soft fur.

Later that afternoon, after the others had left for home, Marishka and I took the kitten out into the garden, where she romped through the grass, chasing every bug and bird that flew overhead. Marishka and I lay on our backs, letting the warm fall sun pour over our faces and arms.

"You're going to have to name the kitten after me," Marishka said suddenly. "That way you won't forget me."

"Why would I forget you?" I replied. "You live just around the corner, silly."

"Not for long, Gabi. We ... my family and I, we're leaving."

"What do you mean, leaving?" I asked, sitting up, a cold knot forming in the pit of my stomach.

"I've been trying to tell you for a long time," said Marishka. "But I didn't know how to say it. And my mother said I couldn't talk too much, in case the soldiers found out and made trouble." Her voice shook slightly. She avoided my stare as she continued talking. "It's not safe here any more, Gabi. You know it and I know it. When we heard about those girls in Levocha who were being taken away, my parents were really upset. And after you and I were almost hurt by that soldier, my mother said it was more than she could stand. We're getting away from here before it's too late."

"Oh, no! Marishka, you can't leave!" I cried. I still couldn't face the fact that we were no longer safe in our homes. Wasn't there anything we could count on any more? "Where are you going?"

"America," she said. "My father has cousins in New York. We'll travel by train to Hungary, then to France, and then by boat across the ocean."

"When?" I whispered.

"As soon as we can. It won't be easy, and we know it's dangerous. There's a railway worker who's willing to hide us in a freight train heading across the border. From there, others are arranging to get us to the coast. I don't know all the details. My parents told me it's costing a lot of money, but it's worth everything we own if we can just get out of here. Gabi, you have to convince your mother to leave too. I know my mother tried to talk to her. But your mother is so stubborn she won't listen."

Who is the stubborn one, I wondered sombrely. I turned to Marishka and hugged her tightly, my eyes brimming with tears.

"I'm naming the cat Mashka," I said, my voice muffled. "But I don't need anything to remind me of you. I'll never forget you! Not ever!"

Later that night, and throughout the next day, Mamma and I talked again and again about Marishka and her family and their reasons for leaving. We knew there were opportunities for us to leave too, and it was time to think seriously about our options. Just a few days before, a cousin of my mother's, living in the United States, had written to encourage us to come and live with her and her family. She promised she could help us get out of the country by supplying us with forged travelling documents that would identify us as Christians. Such papers were nearly impossible to come by, but with the right connections, officials could be bribed. And this cousin somehow had the right connections. Once we were in America, she promised she would help us get settled.

The offers were tempting, especially as we looked around and saw our friends and neighbours leaving. Perhaps we really were being reckless, or just denying the reality around us. And yet, after all the discussions, we still couldn't bring ourselves to go.

We looked at each other and knew what we had to do. In silent agreement, we began to empty out the dresser.

"You never know when a hiding place might come in handy," said Mamma, casually. "It's just as well to be prepared."

Each piece of crystal, china and silver was carefully removed, wrapped in cloth and placed in another cupboard. Even the chess set was carried off to be stored elsewhere. The shelf in the middle of the dresser was lowered to the bottom to make extra space. When we had finished, I looked inside the dresser. It was empty and dark, like a small cave. Would this meagre space be enough to protect me the day I needed it?

That night, as I climbed into bed, I glanced once more out the bedroom window. At night I couldn't see the mountains. Everything looked black and shapeless. But if I moved closer to the window, and strained my neck upward, I could see the line of stars marking the boundary between mountains and sky. Was there a safer place out there for Mamma and me? Such a vastness of space outside, and I was trusting my safety to a cubbyhole of a dresser. Would it be enough? The kitten was curled up in a furry ball, asleep at the foot of my bed. What a strange birthday this had been, I thought. And by my next birthday, would we still be together? Would we still be safe?

Chapter Eleven

SOME WEEKS LATER, Mamma decided that I should practise hiding in the dresser. It would be like a dress rehearsal,
she said, a chance to prepare myself in case I ever needed
to hide. I didn't like the idea one bit.

"I don't need to practise hiding in a dresser," I complained. "It's not as if it's difficult. Besides, you said I had
to sweep the kitchen floor and I haven't done that yet." I
tried every excuse to distract her from making me climb
inside the dresser.

"You must give it a try, Gabi," she insisted. "What if
the dresser is too small for you, or there's not enough air
when we close the door? These are things we have to find
out. Otherwise we can't depend on using the dresser as a
hiding place."

Deep down, I knew she was right. I was worried about
how it would feed to be stuffed inside the dresser. And
who could know how long the soldiers might stay in the
house, searching for me? If I was inside the dresser for a
long time, would there be enough air to breathe? How

scary would it be alone in the dark? What if I needed to stretch and I couldn't? All these questions had been circling inside my head. The only way I would come close to finding out the answers would be to get inside the dresser and see for myself. But the thought of climbing inside was terrifying.

"Maybe we should just forget the whole thing," said Mamma. "It's probably a bad idea for you to stay in this house anyway. And the dresser is such an obvious hiding place. It's probably the first place they would look. What was I thinking when I let you talk me into this? I know you'll be safer if I send you away."

This thought was even more frightening. "Mamma, you promised you wouldn't do that! You promised!"

"Then we have to be prepared. And the only way to do that is for you to practise hiding. There is no other option, Gabi. Either climb inside the dresser, or we get you away from here."

Mamma's threat sounded cruel, but I knew I had no choice. I walked to the dresser and she held the door open for me.

We had already talked about how to handle the emergency, if it ever came. Mamma said that, if we got word that soldiers were coming to look for me, I would have to drop whatever I was doing and run for the dresser. I told her it would be like the fire drills we used to have at school. We had to stop everything we were doing and move outside, and not take our coats or boots or anything else with us. We had been taught to get to safety quickly, and that was what I would have to do here. Once I was inside the dresser, Mamma said I would have to be as quiet as possible. If I moved too much, or coughed or sneezed, I might be heard.

I bent to peer inside the dresser. Without all our beautiful things inside, it didn't look so cosy and inviting. It looked dark and barren. Taking a deep breath, I crawled into the hole. It was cramped and uncomfortable. Even with the shelf lowered, there was barely enough room for me. I had to sit hunched over, clasping my knees to my chest and bending my head forward.

"I'm going to close the door now," said Mamma. "Try to stay inside until I unlock the door and let you out."

As the door slowly closed, the light from outside disappeared until the inside of the dresser was pitch black. It reminded me of that moment every night when I turned out the lights in my room and for a split second I didn't know where I was. But unlike my room, where everything eventually came back into focus, nothing here in the dresser felt familiar. I could not even see my fingers when I held my hand in front of my face. Straining my eyes, I tried to reach out and find something to hold onto, something warm and reassuring. But, the wood surrounding me was rough and hard to my touch, and the isolation was unbearable.

Within minutes I felt the air inside me being sucked away until I could barely breathe. I began to panic. I tried taking deep breaths to calm myself, but it was no use. The more I told myself to relax, the more desperate I felt. And the more desperate I felt, the more hysterical I became. My face became hot, and I was trembling. In my panic my arms began to flail, crashing against the sides of the dresser. My head banged hard against the roof, sending a jolt through my body. By now I was sweating and gulping for air. This was impossible. I couldn't stay in here.

"Let me out!" I yelled, banging my fists against the door. "Open the doors, I have to get out!" I yelled even louder. I heard the grating of the key in the lock, and the doors opened at last.

I was hysterical as I fell to the ground, rubbing the welt already forming on my head. "I can't do it, Mamma! I can't stay there! I can't breathe, I can't see, and I can't move!" I covered my face with my hands and sobbed uncontrollably.

Moments passed as Mamma stared at me. I knew what

she was thinking. She was trying to figure out how she could get me to go and stay with the Kos family in the mountains. I had proved that this plan was a failure, so now we had to do something else. But, I couldn't let her do that. There was no way on earth I was going to leave Mamma. Even if it meant I had to stay in the dresser for days!

"Mamma, I'm sorry, but I just got scared. I didn't think it was going to be so dark or so hot in there. But now it's all right. I know what to expect. Just give me a couple of days and we'll practise again. I promise I'll do better next time. You'll see." I didn't sound convincing even to myself. I knew I was rambling, but somehow I had to make her believe that I would be able to hide inside the dresser when the time came. She looked very doubtful.

"I don't know, Gabi. This isn't something we can fool around with. I have to know that when you climb inside the dresser you can stay there. If I can't be sure of that, then we have to make other plans, right now."

"I promise I'll do better next time, you'll see. Just give me a few days to rest and we'll try again. Please, Mamma."

She suddenly looked tired. The truth was that neither of us had any way of knowing what the best plan was.

"All right, Gabi," she finally said. "We'll wait a few days, and try again."

Chapter Twelve

THE SECOND CHANCE to practise never came. In fact, crazy as it sounds, months went by and we almost forgot about me hiding in the dresser. The news about raids and people being taken away pretty much stopped during this time. Apparently, local people and government officials had started to complain about the disappearance of Jewish doctors, lawyers and business people. In the face of these complaints, the campaign of persecution slowed down for a period of time. That's not to say that the restrictions and discrimination ended. We were still not allowed to go to school, food was still hard to come by and looting was still a regular occurrence.

Occasionally, Mamma would say I should practise hiding in the dresser again. She even suggested having someone come over to see if there was a way to create air holes in the back, so I could breathe better inside. But every time she mentioned anything like that, I managed to distract her and change the topic. It was almost as if we had convinced ourselves that the problems were over and that life would soon return to normal. In fact, our lives did slip into a kind of routine, in spite of everything happening around us. So it came as an even bigger shock when the nightmare suddenly arrived.

I was alone at home, playing with the kitten in the front yard. Mamma had gone to Marishka's house to see if she could find any clothing for us. Marishka's family had left a week earlier, taking only enough clothes and belongings to make the journey overseas to America. They had left everything else behind.

It had taken them a long time for them to gather the necessary travel papers. The longer Marishka remained in our village, the more I tried to convince myself that she might not go. But finally the day had come for her departure. I tried telling her that her family was crazy to leave. But who was I to think I could change her mind? In the end, we vowed that somehow we would see each other again in the future.

Before saying goodbye, Marishka's mother had made us promise to go through the house and take whatever we needed. Mamma had left early in the morning and, though she always worried when she left me alone, I had assured her that I would be fine.

The kitten was chasing butterflies as usual, and I laughed each time she leapt in the air, trying in vain to capture just one unsuspecting creature. I was so involved in my play that I barely heard Mamma's voice calling in the distance.

"Gabi! The soldiers! The trucks! They're coming now! Run and hide!" I turned to see Mamma rushing up the path to the house, fear and panic etched in her face. At first I didn't understand what she was saying. Was this a joke? Was she pretending so that I would be forced to practise hiding again? Then I thought that maybe she had hurt herself, or something had happened to someone else. As she reached the house and shouted again, I realized that this was the real thing. The danger we had been dreading was on our doorstep.

"Gabi! No time to lose. You must hide in the dresser."

The full impact of what she was saying began to sink in, and for a moment I couldn't move. I felt as if my legs were glued to the ground, and I thought crazily that the soldiers were going to find me there, stuck, unable to get away. I shook my head in a daze. Hide, I thought. I've got to hide. I reached for the kitten, but Mamma pulled my arms away.

"No, Gabi. There's no time for the kitten. Leave her here." She grabbed my hand and yanked me towards the house. Together we headed for the dining room and ran to the dresser. Mamma got there first and opened the door, motioning me to climb inside. I hesitated for a moment, peering into the darkness, remembering the disastrous practice a few months earlier.

My first thought was that I couldn't do it. My body stiffened as I remembered how dark and cramped the dresser had been. Beads of sweat broke out on my forehead and upper lip as I recalled how hot and crushed I had felt. Shaking with fear, I wondered if I was going to faint. How could I possibly climb inside the dresser and stay there?

But I had no choice. This was my only chance for safety. At any minute the soldiers would burst through the door, and once they arrived, there would be no hope for me. I was certain to be taken away. My choice was to face the soldiers or face the darkness.

"Hurry, hurry!" Mamma shouted again. "Inside, and not a sound." I had never seen her so frightened. Taking a deep breath, I bent my head and crawled into the dresser. As I settled into the darkness, Mamma quickly closed the door behind me. I heard the sound of the key turning in the lock. I shut my eyes tightly, held my breath and tried to control the rapid beating of my heart.

The dresser felt even worse than the last time. Why hadn't we thought of putting a pillow in here, or something else soft for me to hold onto? There was nothing here except wood and nails. I hugged my body for comfort, but it wasn't enough. I thought to myself, if I scream, Mamma will come and get me. She'll open the door and hold me. I needed air but there wasn't any. Maybe if I opened the door for just a minute, and took a deep breath and then closed the door again, I would feel better. What was I thinking of? This jumble of thoughts was crazy. I knew I couldn't do anything. The soldiers were coming and I had to stay put.

It wasn't long before I heard a muffled pounding at the front door of our house. Harsh, deep voices were talking but I couldn't make out the words. Occasionally the voices grew louder, mixed with the sound of Mamma saying something I couldn't understand. I thought I heard someone say "girl" and then "search," but I couldn't be sure. It sounded as if a lot of people were in the house. I could hear cupboard doors opening and closing. Every now and then I thought I heard a crash, as if something had broken.

My eyes were still closed, my ears straining to make

sense of the sounds outside. My heart was beating so loud and fast that I thought it was going to come right out through my chest. What if someone outside heard? My breathing was quick and shallow as I gulped in tiny mouthfuls of air. I knew that if I didn't slow down my breathing, I was in danger of passing out. Sweat was pouring from my upper lip and forehead. I've got to relax, I thought hopelessly, as I buried my head deep in my chest.

I was frantically worried about Mamma and her safety. What would the soldiers do if they didn't find me? Would they take her instead? Would they hurt her? Then, as I heard voices moving closer to the dresser, I panicked and thought they had found me. What would the soldiers do once they got their hands on me? I knew I would be taken away, but where? Would I be harmed? Would I ever see Mamma again? Each minute felt like a lifetime. It was unbearable to be inside the dresser, and even more unbearable not to know what was happening outside. I hugged my knees closer to my chest and prayed this ordeal would end soon.

Suddenly, I heard something at the door of the dresser. What was that noise? It sounded like sandpaper rubbing against the wood, or some kind of scratching. The soldiers hadn't left yet, so I knew it wasn't Mamma coming to free me. Was it a soldier? Had I been discovered? Maybe Mamma had been right after all, the dresser was too obvious a place to hide. I waited a moment, thinking the door would open, but it didn't. Yet the scratching continued. And then I heard a faint mew and I knew what it was. Mashka! The kitten must have seen me crawl into the dresser, and now she was coming to sniff me out! For one second I forgot my panic and nearly laughed out loud at the craziness of it all. Here I was, thinking that soldiers were about to break into the dresser to find me, when in fact my own little kitten was about to betray me, by scratching and mewing at the door. What a ridiculous way to be discovered!

The moment of humour didn't last long. Within seconds, the sound of Mashka's scratching was replaced by the clumping of boots moving closer and closer. Now I knew my time was up. At any moment they would demand that Mamma open the dresser door. The wave of panic returned full force, and I clenched my fists to my face, biting hard on my hand to stop from screaming out loud. I closed my eyes again and prayed silently for my safety.

And then, in the darkness of my hiding place, I became aware of something close to me. At first I felt something warm, as if strong arms were reaching out to surround me. I opened my eyes and peered into the murky shadows. I couldn't see a thing, but I still felt something there. As I turned my head to the left and right I sensed it again and again. I couldn't quite describe the feeling. Was it a smell? Like shaving lotion? No, perhaps the faint odour of a pipe. It was achingly familiar, and it filled the corners of the dresser until I finally realized what it was. Papa! His smell, his smile. Outside the dresser, the shuffling and pounding of the soldiers' search continued. But inside the dresser I felt the warmth of Papa's gaze on my face, and slowly I felt my body begin to relax. The rapid beating of my heart slowed down. My breathing became quieter and more even. My fears began to disappear. It was as if Papa were there with me, to protect me as he had done when he was alive. I heard him speak, and I listened to his comforting voice:

I will shelter you from harm,
You must have no fear,
You'll be safe, my precious child,
You'll be safe, my dear.

Over and over I heard Papa's voice repeating the poem. And each time I heard the poem, and each time I saw Papa's smile, I felt myself grow calmer and calmer. The voices outside the dresser were now just a muffled hum in the distance. The darkness around me no longer felt cold. The wooden floor of the dresser seemed to cushion me. I felt warm and protected. I knew I would be safe.

Chapter Thirteen

I DON'T KNOW how long I stayed like that in the dresser, but hours must have passed before I heard the sound of the key in the lock and felt a rush of fresh air as the door opened. I tumbled out, head first into Mamma's arms. She grabbed me and pulled me close. We hugged tightly while I sobbed with relief.

"There, there, my Gabilinka. It's over. The soldiers are gone and you are safe." Mamma rocked me in her arms, stroking my hair and face. I was drenched with sweat, and strands of wet hair clung to my face and neck. My sobs were loud and aching, and my relief at seeing Mamma was mixed with the agonizing memory of what I had just been through. Mamma kissed my forehead, whispering over and over, "You are safe. The soldiers are gone." Even though her voice was soothing, I could tell from her trembling arms that she had been as terrified as I had been.

It was many minutes before my racing heart slowed and I could catch my breath. Pulling away from Mamma's arms, I looked around the sitting room, realizing what a shambles the house was. Clothing and linen were scattered everywhere. Dishes from the kitchen cupboards were broken or lying in piles on the floor. Glasses were shattered. Plants were knocked over. Even the carpets had been pulled up. It looked as if a cyclone had hit the house. Nothing was in its place. Then, from under a pile of pillows, I heard a soft scratching and a muffled cry.

"Mashka, my poor baby," I called, reaching under the pillows to retrieve the whimpering kitten. "The soldiers didn't get you either!" I held the kitten close to my face while she purred, and her rough tongue brushed against my cheek, licking away the traces of sweat and tears. After many more minutes I was finally calm enough to listen to Mamma describe what had happened in the house while I was hiding.

The soldiers had marched up the path to the house only seconds after Mamma locked the door to the dresser. Pounding on the door, they demanded to know if any young girls lived in the house. Mamma calmly told them that, yes, she had a daughter, but that I was away, visiting relatives in the country. She knew even as she spoke that they didn't believe her. They yelled that she was lying, and roughly pushed their way inside. The soldier who was in charge ordered the others to begin tearing apart the house, looking for me.

Mamma's eyes closed as she described how they had ransacked every corner and every cupboard searching room by room. Furniture was shoved out of place and the contents of closets were strewn across the floor. The linen chest was overturned so that the hinges on the lid broke. The sugar bowl was smashed, and sugar crunched beneath their boots. The carpets were ripped up in case there was a trap door leading to a hiding place underneath the house. Lamps had been pushed over and pictures shifted out of place. The coffee table was overturned along with a bookshelf, scattering dozens of books across the sitting room floor. The soldiers' search had been thorough and sweeping. How could they have overlooked the dresser?

"They searched such a long time, and they found nothing," said Mamma. "And they were getting tired and impatient, and I thought they were about to give up, when suddenly your little kitten came running into the sitting room crying for you. She walked straight to the dresser and began scratching at the door. I thought I was going to faint." Tears gathered in Mamma's eyes at the memory of her terror. "One of the soldiers, a young one, noticed the kitten and headed for the dresser. It was as if he suddenly realized that it was there, and that it hadn't been searched. I didn't know what to do. I thought for sure they would find you."

"How did you stop them?" I asked.

"Well, you won't believe this, Gabilinka, but just then I remembered something I once saw in a movie. The character in the movie was trying to get people on the street to look at her, so they wouldn't notice her friend stealing from a store. In the middle of the street she started yelling and yelling, and everyone ran towards her to see what was happening. I thought of this scene at the exact moment the soldier was walking towards the dresser, so I started yelling and wailing like a crazy woman. I fell to my knees, screaming that all my beautiful things were being destroyed. Oh, you should have seen me! What a performance I gave them! And best of all, I scared the kitten away from the dresser!"

I had to smile as Mamma described the scene. I pictured her on the floor, her hands thrashing in the air, her frantic shrieks cutting through the soldiers' ears.

"And it worked! The soldier who was heading for the dresser was distracted and started towards me instead. I never knew I was such a good actress!" She tossed her head back and laughed. "They couldn't think what to do with me. The soldier who was in charge threatened to beat me and told the young one to get me out of the living room. He dragged me into the kitchen, but I kept on yelling and screaming.

"Finally the one in charge appeared again, only this time he was holding my jewellery box. Remember when that letter came, saying that all Jews had to turn over their jewellery to the authorities? Well, I never told you, Gabi, but I didn't hand mine in. I knew I was breaking the law, but I hid my treasures in a box under a loose floorboard in my room. When he came in with that box, I thought I was going to be arrested for sure. Instead, he said that because I had annoyed him with my screaming, he was going to take the box and everything in it, and there was nothing I could do about it."

"Oh, Mamma!" I cried. "Not your jewellery! Not your wonderful pearls and everything!" Mamma's jewellery had been passed down through several generations. Her gold bracelets and necklaces, and her sapphire earrings and her ruby brooch, were inherited from her mother and grand-mother. Other favourite pieces of jewellery had been gifts from Papa. They had meant so much to her, and to me. And now they were all gone.

"Gabi, they are trinkets," said Mamma, smiling. "They

are meaningless next to our lives and your safety. Anyway, once the soldiers found the jewellery, they seemed to lose interest in searching. They went away shortly after that, leaving the house as you see it now. I waited a half-hour more before letting you out of the dresser, to make sure they wouldn't come back."

We hugged once more. It was a miracle that I hadn't been discovered. It was a miracle that Mamma hadn't been harmed. That was when I noticed her hand.

"Mamma, you're bleeding!" I exclaimed, grabbing her by the wrist. "Did the soldiers hurt you?"

"No," she assured me. "It was the key. When I locked you in the dresser, I had no time to hide the key. I was afraid that if I put it down, the soldiers might find it. And if I put it in my pocket, it might fall out. So I just kept it in my hand. I must have held it so tightly that it cut into my palm."

I examined her hand closely. Indeed, on her palm there were deep red indentations tracing the outline of the key to the dresser, and cuts where the jagged edges had broken the skin. The bloody marks defined how fiercely she had protected me — how much she loved me.

"Someone must be watching over us," she murmured.

"Yes," I replied. "And I know who."

I told Mamma about the feeling I had had that Papa was looking out for me while I hid in the dresser. I told her how I could almost see him, and smell his clothes and his shaving lotion. I described how terrified I had been when I first crawled into the dresser and the door had closed on me, and how my fears had begun to disappear when I felt Papa's closeness. I told her it was as if Papa were in there with me. And I recited the poem I had heard whispered to me in the darkness of my hiding place.

Mamma listened carefully to everything I said. As I finished reciting Papa's poem, she smiled.

"Yes, my darling, I believe you're right. Papa is indeed watching over us. And I feel much better knowing he's there."

Chapter Fourteen

As soon as we pulled ourselves together, Mamma and I began to clean up the house. Mamma said she couldn't stand to look at the mess left by the soldiers. Every piece of furniture out of place, every broken dish and glass, was a reminder that the house had been invaded and ransacked. We had to put it all back in order so we could start to feel at home again.

We quickly set about straightening the carpets, rearranging the furniture, throwing out the broken dishes, and moving everything else back to where it belonged. Within a short period of time the downstairs was looking almost like its old self. But try as we might, we couldn't rid the house of the memories left by the raid. Every time I closed my eyes I could hear boots on the path outside. I could hear angry voices shouting threats at Mamma, and I could see the soldiers destroying our belongings. Long after the rooms had been tidied up, I still felt there were defiling marks on everything in our home.

Everything, that is, except the dresser. No one had

touched the dresser. It had been my good luck charm, my sanctuary; the best hiding place we could have found.

Of all the rooms in the house, my bedroom was in the worst mess. The soldiers had done a particularly thorough job of searching it. Perhaps they thought they might find some clue to my whereabouts. Every single cupboard, drawer and closet had been emptied. Clothes were scattered everywhere. My precious books lay in a heap on the floor. My bed was a shambles. I picked up the bedspread from the floor and watched, horrified, as my china doll, the doll Nina had once given me for my birthday, fell out from under the covers.

The doll lay on the floor, her porcelain face shattered, her embroidered clothing torn and dirty. Next to the doll, on the carpet, was a single black boot mark.

I sank to the floor and gathered the doll in my arms, hugging her close. She was destroyed, and her smashed face was a cruel reminder that my friendship with Nina was broken, and that the whole life I had known in this place was shattered and beyond repair. I was still sitting there on the floor when Mamma came in. She nodded sympathetically towards the doll as she sat gently on the edge of my bed.

"Gabi," she began clearing her throat. "Do you

remember when we talked about the Kos family, who used to work on our farm?"

"You mean the family who moved back up to the mountains?" I replied nervously. The last time Mamma had talked about the Kos family had been when she was thinking of sending me away. My heart grew cold as I waited to hear what she was going to say next.

"That's right. They are good people and they always said we could turn to them for help. Well, I think it's time to talk about going to stay with them ..."

"No!" I interrupted. "Absolutely not! Mamma, we had this conversation before. I told you then and I'm telling you now, I am *not* leaving here without you." As angry as I sounded, deep down in my heart I was terrified that she would give me no choice. If she decided that I had to leave, there would be nothing I could do. "Do you understand what I'm saying, Mamma?" I pleaded. "Please don't send me away!"

"Gabi, my darling, calm down and let me finish," continued Mamma. "I'm not just talking just about *you* going to stay with the Kos family. I'm talking about *us*. It's time to talk about both of us going to hide somewhere together."

I was stunned. On the one hand, it was a relief to know that Mamma no longer meant to send me away. If we went, we would go together. On the other hand, she was actually thinking we should leave our home.

"I didn't tell you this, Gabi," she added, "but the soldiers were furious that they didn't find you. When they were about to leave, the one in charge said he would be back. And the next time he came, he said he would be coming for me." She took my hand and held it in hers. "The truth is, neither of us is safe here any more."

Mamma was right. And so was Marishka's family. And so were the Bottensteins and the Wohls and the Singers and everyone else who had escaped our village. It was senseless to stay any longer. No Jewish family was safe here. The danger was too great. If we had to leave our homes to protect our lives then that was what we had to do.

"Who knows how long this madness will last?" said Mamma sadly. "But one thing is for certain. We can't wait here for it to end."

"When will we leave?" I asked.

"As soon as we have packed a few necessities," she replied. "It may take some time to arrange things. But I will send word to the Kos family that we need their help. As soon as we receive their reply and the arrangements are in place, we will go."

I looked around my room, knowing I wouldn't be able to take much with me. Maybe it was better that way. If I had to choose only a few things, the choice would be next to impossible. Nearly everything in my room was precious to me. I remembered the game Marishka and I used to play on our way to school. What ten things would we take if we had to leave the country? The doll had always been my first choice, but she was destroyed. I looked at Mashka sleeping peacefully at the foot of my bed. I would convince Mamma to let me take the kitten along with us. She would be happy there. She was strong and clever, she would be all right wherever she was. I knew the same was true of Mamma and me. I sighed deeply.

"Don't look so worried, my darling," said Mamma as she stood to leave my room. "We have managed to stay safe so far. And I'm sure we'll continue to be safe. You're the one who always reminded me to remember what Papa used to say: everything will be all right as long as we're together. So together we will be."

"Will we ever come back, Mamma?"

"Who knows, my darling? Who knows?"

Chapter Fifteen

"DID YOU EVER GO BACK, Babichka?" Paul asked as the story ended. Vera and Paul were still lying on the couch in their grandmother's living room. Their grandmother had been talking for several hours, and outside it was already beginning to grow dark. Soon, Vera and Paul's parents would be arriving to take them home after their long day's visit. Inside the living room, the lamp cast a soft, light shadow over the face of their grandmother and over the surface of the dresser which stood behind her.

"Well, let me tell you what happened in the end," she replied. "My mother and I did leave our home to hide in the mountains with the Kos family. We hid in their barn, and each day they would bring us food, water and other things we needed. They had a daughter my age, named Evichka, and we became friends and often played together in the haystacks of the barn. The days were long and often boring for me. I don't know what I would have done without Evichka's companionship.

"Sometimes my mother allowed me to borrow some of

Evichka's clothes. When I was dressed as a village child, I was allowed to play outside with Evichka at night, when it was dark and there was little chance of us being seen. We could go outside only if we stayed close to the barn. Outside I felt free, and I could breathe the fresh air. All the same, even at night it was daring and risky for me to leave our hiding place. If anyone in the village had seen us and become suspicious, we might have been reported to the police, and we would have been arrested instantly. Eventually it became too dangerous to go outside the barn. Soldiers were roaming through these villages, searching for hidden Jewish families. And some of the peasants were eager to turn us in. So most of the time I just stayed hidden in the barn, playing games with Mamma and Evichka, or reading books the family brought us.

"I was thirteen and a half when Mamma and I went to hide in that barn in the mountains, and fifteen when the war ended and we knew it was safe to return to our village. We had been away almost a year and a half. The time had seemed endless.

"It was difficult to say goodbye to Evichka and her family at the end of the war. They had risked their lives to keep us safe. I stayed in touch with Evichka for years after that, writing occasional letters, until we finally lost touch.

But I shall never forget her family's kindness and courage.

"Mamma and I travelled down the mountain to our home, not knowing what we would find there. Well, our house was still there, looking very much as we had left it. But there was one big change. Another family was living in it! Can you imagine what it was like to come home after so long and find that the home we thought was ours no longer belonged to us? It was like that with so many Jewish families. Strangers had simply taken over our houses. And the law had let them do it. Our furniture, our books, our personal belongings, were all being used by strangers. And there was not one thing we could do about it!

"I remember when Mamma and I knocked on the door of our house. The woman who answered was the wife of the supervisor who had come to oversee our property when we were still living there. She knew instantly who we were, and she was clearly embarrassed. We knew she was worried that we might try to make trouble for her, so she let us come in and take a few special treasures. Mamma took her silver candlesticks, the chessboard that Papa and I used to play on, and a few other items that were important to her. Then she faced the woman who now lived in our house and demanded one single piece of furniture. Can you guess what it was? Of course, it was the dresser.

This beautiful dresser that you see here in my living room was the one piece Mamma was determined not to leave behind.

"The other woman was startled, but Mamma was so firm with her that she had no choice but to agree. Mamma borrowed an old truck and we used it to move the dresser and the other small things. For several months after that, we stayed with cousins in a town close by. Then, with our meagre belongings, Mamma and I made our way across the ocean to begin our new lives in North America."

Silence settled upon the living room as the story ended. Vera and Paul looked in amazement at the dresser that stood before them. Slowly they rose from the couch and approached the dresser, opening its doors to peer inside. Paul crouched down, measuring his own height against the height of the dresser. He wondered what it would feel like to have to stay curled up like that, inside that small, dark space for hours and hours.

"Babichka," Vera said thoughtfully, "Gabi — I mean, *you* were so brave. I don't know if I could have hidden in there."

"Well," replied her grandmother, "I was scared. But I had my Papa there to protect me. At least, I felt I did. And each time I heard his voice, I was a little less frightened."

"And that helped you?" asked Vera doubtfully.

"It helped me very much. Sometimes, when you believe that someone or something is there to help you, it makes you feel you can do anything."

"Like the time you gave me that lucky penny to hold, when I auditioned for the play at school?"

"That's exactly right. The penny was a reminder of me. And when you held the penny and thought of me, it gave you courage for your audition. In the same way, my papa's voice was a reminder of him. And when I thought of him and imagined his voice, his presence, I felt calm and brave."

"Still, I hope I never have to have that much courage," sighed Vera.

For a moment Gabi Kohn didn't reply. She knew she had been lucky to survive the war, when so many others hadn't. She prayed silently that her children and grand-children would never have to suffer the way her people had been made to suffer during those terrible times.

"Oh, I hope so too," she replied. "But listen, I think I hear your parents knocking. Come, let's open the door for them, and have a quick bite to eat before you all go home."

Later that evening, long after Vera and Paul and their

parents had left, Gabi Kohn walked through the darkened hallway of her home into the living room. Alone in her house, she approached the dresser. She ran her hand lovingly across the old wood, now faded and rough with age.

Slowly she opened the door of the dresser, the door that had once been opened for her to crawl inside and hide. She peered into its dark interior and thought of her father, as she had thought of him so many times since that day. She still missed him; that would never change. But once again she saw his smile, and heard his brave and wonderful words:

I will shelter you from harm,
You must have no fear,
You'll be safe, my precious child,
You'll be safe, my dear.

Author's Note

Most of the characters and incidents in *The Secret of Gabi's Dresser* are fictional. However, the historical setting is accurate, and the story is inspired by real people and a real event. During the Second World War, my mother hid in a wooden dresser that was in her mother's dining room. While she hid, soldiers from the Slovak Guard searched the house looking for her. Her mother, my grandmother, reportedly held the key to the dresser so tightly in her hand that her palm bled from its indentation. My mother's brother, who was just a young boy at the time, was able to distract the guards and divert their attention from my mother's hiding place. For the purpose of the narrative, he is not included in *The Secret of Gabi's Dresser*. However, in real life he played a key role in saving my mother from being discovered.

By 1944, the German army was deporting all remaining Jewish families in eastern Slovakia to concentration camps. In the face of increasing danger, my mother and her family left their home to hide in a small mountain village close to the Polish border. There they remained until the end of the war when that village was liberated by Russian soldiers. They travelled back to their hometown where my grandmother retrieved the dresser and brought it with her, first to Israel where they lived for several years, and then to North America. The dresser sat in my grandmother's dining room until her death in 1989, when she left it to me. It now sits in the dining room of my home.

My grandmother as a young woman.

*My mother as a young girl of
about six years.*

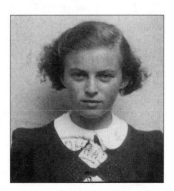

*My mother at about thirteen years of age —
the same age as the Gabi in this story
was when she hid in the dresser.*

My grandmother and mother standing in a garden. This picture was taken in 1941 and shows them in happier times.

Three years later, in 1944, these two pictures were taken outside the barn in the small mountain village where my mother and grandmother hid. They are dressed in peasant clothing borrowed from the villagers.

The War in Czechoslovakia

September 1938
Germany, Great Britain, France and Italy sign the Munich Pact, which turns the western part of Czechoslovakia, known as Sudetenland, over to Germany.

March 1939
Slovakia, in the eastern part of the country, declares its independence and signs a Treaty of Protection with Nazi Germany. While the country has been divided, leaving eastern Slovakia independent, both parts are equally committed to persecuting the Jewish people.

June 1939
A list of anti-Jewish laws is proclaimed. Over the next few years, more and more restrictions are brought in against Jews.

October 1939
The first Czech Jews are deported to concentration camps in Poland. By October 1942, 75 percent of Czech Jews have been deported. Most of them are killed at the Auschwitz concentration camp.

September 1941
The Jewish Code is established. It lists 270 paragraphs of restrictions against Jews.

February 1942
The deportation of Jews from Slovakia begins. Poor shopkeepers and innkeepers are deported first, followed by political people, young single girls and, finally, whole families.

1942 – 1944
The Jews of Slovakia continue to be deported to concentration camps. The government of Slovakia pays Germany for every Jew deported. Of the 137,000 Jews in pre-war Slovakia, more than 72,000 die in death camps.

May 1945
Allied soldiers liberate Czechoslovakia.